At the House of the

Magician

Also by Mary Hooper

At the House of the
Magician

MARY HOOPER

BLOOMSBURY

LONDON BERLIN NEW YORK SYDNEY

Bloomsbury Publishing, London, Berlin, New York and Sydney

Published in Great Britain in 2007 by Bloomsbury Publishing Plc
50 Bedford Square, London, WC1B 3DP

Illustrations by Carol Lawson

A CIP catalogue record for this book is available from the British Library

ISBN 978 0 7475 8886 3

MIX
Paper from
responsible sources
FSC® C018072
FSC
www.fsc.org

Printed in Great Britain by Clays Ltd, St Ives Plc

7 9 10 8

www.bloomsbury.com/childrens
www.maryhooper.co.uk

For Kevin and Stephen with love

Contents

Chapter One

I found myself a tidy selling space at the edge of the common, almost upon the hawthorn hedge. On the other side was a shorn field which the geese had been let into to go a-stubbling and begin fattening themselves for Christmas, and as I unpacked my lavender wands I could hear them calling to each other, pecking and scratching on the dry earth, occasionally flapping their wings to try and keep themselves cool.

I shook out a clean linen cloth and spread it over the grass, flattening the daisies and goldcups as I did so, humming a ballad to myself. It was the beginning of September and, being Michelmas Fair in our village, a day of merry-making, I was happy as I set out my wares. I knew I was sure to sell all the lavender wands I'd made and I intended to buy myself something very fine to wear with the money.

Next to me was Harriet Simon, who had a bench on

the grass holding a selection of her biscuits. 'Crispy sugar jumbales!' I could hear her calling under her breath, practising in readiness for the customers. 'Oh, sweet jumbales!' Beside her was Old Mistress Roberts, selling lucky charms made of seashells, and next along a housewife selling eggs and flummeries, then a quack doctor with a table bearing a selection of differently coloured bottles: cordials, tinctures, lotions and potions. I couldn't read the banner which flew above his head, but Harriet could and told me that he claimed to cure any illness known to man, and some which were not known.

There were countless other stalls and peddlers about the field, but it was only me who was selling lavender wands. Seventeen of these I'd made, each containing twenty-one long stalks of lavender bent backwards over their flowers and woven around with lengths of emerald, scarlet or white ribbon and tied in a bow. I'd have liked more to sell, but had only enough space for six small lavender bushes, and these I'd had to hide away in odd places around our cottage: at the centre of a towering column of beans, at the back of the shed or in the shade of a monstrous cabbage. This was because my father wouldn't have anything in the garden which didn't pay its way and he, being merry with ale one night, had found and uprooted three of my precious young plants and thrown them to the pig to eat. (I pause and ponder here why they always say that a man is merry with ale when it seems to me that

Father is never merry when he's been drinking, but only more ill-tempered than usual.)

The lavender did pay its way, of course, but Father didn't know that. He didn't know that every year since I'd been a small child I'd been tending my lavender bushes, picking the stems at just the right moment before the flowers opened and drying them by hanging them in bunches in the sunshine. The money I made by selling my wands I always divided into three: with the first I bought something pretty to wear, the next part went to Ma to spend as she saw fit, the last was kept to buy ribbons for the wands I'd make the following year.

Lady Ashe, who is high-born and speaks very grand, opened the day's festivities. Lady Ashe is the wife of Sir Reginald Ashe, the Lord of the Manor, and had, in times past, been lady-in-waiting to our good Queen Elizabeth. I oft thought of how exciting her life must have been then, for Milady was at court when the queen and she were girls, and she must have many tales to tell of the intrigues of courtly life, of conspiracies, unrequited love, dancing and minstrels. And imagine attending on the queen! Surely no other position and no other way of life could be more pleasing or more delightful? As I thought *that*, I felt for the little token I always wear round my neck. My family oft tease me about this trinket, for 'tis but a groat with a hole bored in it (and not even a real groat, for it's been falsely coined and makes my neck black in the hot weather). It bears a profile of our queen, however, stamped on to the metal, and such is my devotion to Her Grace that I wear it constantly.

Lady Ashe still dresses very fine and on the day of the Fair was wearing a red silk dress with jewelled bodice and great collar of lace, and so amazing was this latter garment that I felt compelled to draw close to where she was standing in order to admire it the better. The collar stood out at each side of her neck much like wings, or the eaves of a house, each wing being covered in delicate embroidery and edged into wired points, and each point having on it a droplet of gold which shivered and swung as she moved. Her hair was piled high and twisted around with pearls, roped together, and her face was very white, as if polished with the same pearl lustre.

She was a plain woman, but her glittering jewels and decorations gave her a kind of beauty and every other woman there looked dowdy by comparison. I felt especially drab, for my bodice and skirt, although made of fine lawn in a pretty shade of apple green, had been handed on to me by my sister and was horridly out of fashion. I gazed at Lady Ashe in admiration and envy. If only, I thought, one of those gold teardrops could fall from her collar and drop to the floor! With just one of these (for I well knew the worth of such a thing) I'd be able to release my youngest brother from his bonded apprenticeship as a coffin-maker, relieve our ma of the burden of her work (for her eyes ached dreadfully now) and buy us a little plot of land of our own. How strange, I thought, that all those things might be purchased by something so small! But I knew that men fought wars and killed their fellows for gold and had heard, too, that great sums were being laid out in order that alchemists might find the subtle powder which was said to change ordinary metals into it.

Lady Ashe exhorted everyone to enjoy the jugglers and the rope-walkers and spend wisely at the stalls, and added that she herself would be attending the hiring fair on Brownlow's Field in order to obtain two or three maids for her household. There was some gasping at this, some preening and patting of hair and some smoothing down of skirts, for many a girl there would have given anything to be taken into service at Hazelgrove Manor. Here, it was said, every one of the servants – even the kitchen maids – slept on mattresses freshly stuffed with lady's bedstraw and had red meat to eat each day. I thought of something else, too, which set my heart pitter-pattering: there was a rumour that the queen herself had come a-visiting Hazelgrove Manor in order to see her old friend Lady Ashe.

When I remembered this, the notion came to me that I might go and be hired as a maid by Milady. It would be a way of getting out of my father's clutches – and besides, I knew I couldn't stay at home for ever. Could I leave my ma, though? How would she manage without me there to do the close-up work? We made gloves for the gentry, and it looked to me as if Lady

Ashe might be wearing a pair of ours, for they were of finest soft blue leather and had smocking around the wrist in a pattern well known to me. If they were of our making, then Ma would have done the cutting out and the tacking together, and I'd have spent any number of hours sewing the slender fingers with stitches so fine and dainty you'd think a faery had worked them.

Perhaps I wouldn't go for hiring this year, but would nevertheless go to Brownlow's Field to see how things proceeded there, to study who got hired and who didn't, for it would be sure to stand me in good stead in the future.

I'd sold all my lavender wands within the hour and, stowing my money carefully in my pocket, folded up Ma's best tablecloth and put it in my basket. Before I went to the hiring, however, I couldn't resist having a look around the stalls to see if there was anything among the trinkets and the gee-gaws and the singing birds that I fell in love with. It was a wonderful feeling to have coins in my pocket, coins that were all mine for the spending, and it only happened once a year, for the money Ma and I earned making gloves went straight to Father. Of course, there were many precious and lovely things on the stalls and many more being carried about by the peddlers, and I went round the field twice and was unable to decide between an embroidered bodice, a canary bird in a wire cage or a thin silvery chain that I could thread my groat on to, for at present it was only hanging round my neck on a length of cord.

I'd think about each of these things, I decided, and in the meantime go to see how the choosing was done at the hiring fair.

Brownlow's Field used to be common land where we could graze animals, but had been enclosed recently with tall brushwood fencing by Squire Brownlow, who owns a big house nearby. There had been some hostility about this enclosing, and one of the village men had tried to lead a protest, but it had come to nothing because Squire Brownlow is rich, owns many acres and employs a lot of villagers, so folk had been reluctant to make a stand against him.

There was a considerable number of people on the field, in the centre of which a rough awning had been erected as shelter from the sun. Under this a fellow was standing playing a violin, and several girls were dancing a jig to its merry refrain. Also under the awning's shelter, standing on boxes, were the folk still waiting to be hired. These were young, mostly, for older folk tend to settle in their jobs for the long term (so Ma had told me) – and besides, are not so good to hire, for the older they are then the less healthy and more like they are to have days off sick.

There was a fair number of servants waiting there, and a greater number of masters, and these intermingled with peddlers crying up refreshments: posset-drinks, rose water, Rhenish wine and raspberry mead. People came from far and near to the hiring fair, for it was only held once a year, and all trades carried something of their line of work about them so they might be easily recognised: the maids had mops; the dairymaids, pails; and cooks carried a wooden spoon or ladle. I also saw thatchers with stooks of corn, a wool-carder with a hank of coloured wool and various ploughmen and other workers of the land.

Their potential employers stood around, sizing them up, talking between themselves and no doubt passing on many a sly word on the virtues – or other-wise – of a certain servant. Now and again an employer would approach one standing on a box and look at their teeth to see if they were healthy, or feel a labour-er's muscles to see if he had the strength to manage a carthorse or drive a plough. One burly fellow – a black-smith, judging by the horseshoe tucked into his hatband – had stripped to the waist to show off his muscles and was drawing approving glances from many of the women there. He was too old for me to admire, however (and besides, seemed to be of a type that Ma oft described as all brawn and no brains). Now and then a deal would be struck along the line; the master would shake hands with the servant and a silver shilling placed in the latter's hand to seal the bargain.

I waited until the fellow with the violin took a pause and the maids had ceased dancing, then asked them if they had already been hired.

'Indeed we have,' said one, retying the ribbons of

her cap and picking up her pail – for she was a dairy-maid. 'I was hired straightaway by a very nice gent'man farmer.' She smiled at me and was very pretty, with deep blue eyes and fair curls, so I knew why she'd been taken so readily.

'And because we are sisters, I was hired too!' said the girl with her.

'Although some poor girls have been standing there an hour or more,' the first whispered, and we glanced at the girls still standing on boxes, some of whom were looking rather discomforted. I couldn't help but notice, however, that those who remained standing were either dull and weak looking, or plump and thus likely to eat a lot and be costly to keep.

'But you don't carry anything with you. What's your trade?' asked the pretty one.

'I'm a glove-maker,' I said, 'but I don't want to do that all my life.' I looked along the line of girls wistfully. 'Perhaps I could be a seamstress, though – or a maid of all work.'

'I fear the best places are gone,' said the other.

'Has Lady Ashe been in?' I asked.

They nodded. 'She took three girls!'

'Oh.' I nodded ruefully. I'd not been prepared, though. Not thought enough about it beforehand, or asked Ma's opinion on the subject.

'The thing to do is get here early,' said the first, 'and then you can have your pick. If someone you don't like the look of wants to hire you, you can say no and wait for someone better.'

'And if no one better comes along, you can tell the first gent'man you've changed your mind!' said her sister.

I thanked them for their advice and went back to the field where the stalls were, for I'd quite made up my mind to buy the silver chain. As I crossed the field the Morris men were dancing and I watched them a while, laughing and clapping their antics. It was then that I felt a hand clasp my shoulder.

There was something in the landing of it: 'twas not a friendly clasp, as between friends, but a heavy grip, every finger pressing into my flesh, and I knew immediately who it must be.

I wheeled around to face him. 'Father!'

'Ah. You might well look affrighted, you devious jade,' said he, swaying slightly on his feet, 'for I hear that unbeknown to me you've taken up as a stallholder.'

I couldn't speak for fear, knowing someone must have seen me and told him about it.

'And what's more, that you have been a-selling of the family property.'

I shook my head. ''Twas hardly that – 'twas just some lavender I rooted and planted myself.'

He shook me, his hand in an iron grip on my left shoulder so that it already felt bruised. 'Planted in *my* ground. And tended in *my* time, when you should have been working with your ma at your gloves.'

I could tell that he'd been at the ale from the slurring of his words and wished with all my heart that I'd already spent the money I'd earned, for I well knew what was coming next.

'But give me what you've made today and I'll say no more about it.'

I considered this. Perhaps if I gave him some of the coins he'd be content – but this would be near-impossible, for the moment he saw the contents of my pocket, he'd be sure to take the lot.

His grip on me tightened. 'I am the head of the house and your lord and master. Remember, anything earned by a member of my house is mine.'

I wasn't brave enough to speak, but I shook my head slightly. This was enough to make him growl in anger.

'Give me what you've got or I'll take it from you, and give you a leathering into the bargain.'

I looked beyond him, measuring the distance to the field gate. I could certainly outrun him – but then my reckoning would come later, at home, and upset Ma. It would be best to hand the money over now and be done with it. And yet I couldn't bring myself to.

His other hand gripped my right shoulder and he shook me backwards and forwards, making my head judder and causing me to bite my tongue. 'Dare you defy me, you little wretch?'

Frightened now, for he was a big man, I actually moved my hand towards my pocket to give up what I'd earned – but something made me stop. To tend my lavender bushes all year, carefully choose the colours of the ribbands, make the wands and then have my precious earnings taken away from me in a moment – it wasn't fair! No, I could not, *would* not do it.

'Do you dare defy me?' he asked. He lifted his hand and gave me a blow across the face which brought tears to my eyes, and suddenly I felt exceeding angry. Was I just going to stand there and be beaten in front of half the village? No, I was not! As he brought his hand back to land me another blow, I wrenched myself from his grip and pushed him away. Dodging clear of his flailing arms I began to run away from him across the field, just avoiding the Morris men and earning myself several curses as a number of them faltered in their dance.

At the field gate I stopped and looked back. My father had not attempted to run after me, but was surveying me, hands on hips, with a sneering, scornful expression. This meant, I knew, that he was not going to bother to expend energy on running after me but would see to me later, at home.

I sped across the village green and down the lane which led to our cottage, impelled to run but wondering what good it would do me. In the end Father would take the money, that was certain. He would take the money and I would have a beating, and whether it came today or tomorrow hardly mattered.

This was my life, and I did not think much of it.

Chapter Two

'You must flee this place,' said Ma, after listening to my tale with a worried frown. 'You must go quickly before he comes back, and I'll say I've not seen you since you left for the Fair this morning.'

I felt tears spring to my eyes and saw responding ones in her own.

''Tis not that I want you to go, Lucy.' She put down the piece of maroon leather she was working on and pulled me close. 'But I fear for you. His temper is such that I'm in terror for your life. I'd stand up to him and protect you if I could . . .'

I shook my head. 'That wouldn't do any good,' I said, for Ma was small and slight. She had also, the previous evening, been subjected to a blow from my father which had been so violent that it had knocked her to the floor, where he'd kicked her like a dog. Not only that, but she also still wore a blossoming purple bruise to the right side of her face where, last week, he'd thrown a wooden trencher at her.

I buried my face in her blouse. She smelled of soap scented with camomile, of woodsmoke and home. 'I'm frightened, Ma . . .'

'Of him? Of course you are.'

I nodded. 'Of him – and of leaving. Where would I go?'

She thought for a moment. 'Best not to stay around here,' she said. 'Why not try London? They say jobs aplenty can be found there.'

'But what would I do?'

'You could do any one of a hundred different things, Lucy, for you've always been a canny child. You could work as a housemaid, do plain cooking or serve at table. You could take a milch-cow round at doors, cry food in the streets or make potions and simples for an apothecary. There's always work in the city for those who want it.'

'But how would you manage without me?'

Ma stroked my hair. 'I'd be all right, sweeting. And 'twould be enough for me to know that you were out of his way. It's been nothing but bad discourse between you for months now.'

She spoke the truth. Father was a man who wanted his own way – and if he had to bully, cuss or even strike people to get it, then he would. When I was younger his manner had hardly troubled me, for he'd worked long hours on the land and we'd not seen much of him. Two years ago, however, he'd lost his labouring job and was now at home a good deal of the time, where he sat, morbid and complaining, jeering at my tardiness in glove-making (when I was not in the least bit slow) and saying that he'd be lumbered with me for life, for I was too plain to find a husband. When he got a few days' labour and came by money, things got worse, for he'd go straight from the fields to the tavern and arrive home spoiling for a fight.

'Why don't you come with me, Ma?' I urged her now.

She shook her head, smiling slightly. 'I'm too old and worn to beg for my food and sleep o'nights in barns. I'm too old for traipsing to London. Besides, how would everyone manage? How would your sisters fare without me being around to care for their children?'

I sighed, knowing that she spoke truly and that it was a rare day – like today, when most people were at the Fair – that there weren't one or two of my little nieces or nephews hanging at her skirts while my sisters worked. I gave an anxious glance out of the window to make sure that Father wasn't coming down the lane, trying to decide what to do. Was the time to go *now*? Was this the moment I'd been waiting for – could I really leave my home? Other girls from our village had gone away and done well, so we'd heard tell: one had become mistress of a tavern, another worked in a draper's shop selling linens, several had become housemaids.

'If I'd stirred myself earlier today I might have

worked for Lady Ashe,' I said to Ma. 'She was at the hiring fair today.'

Ma shook her head. 'She lives too close by and your pa would discover you were there and come and seek you out. He'll never come to London, though.'

I shook my head. "Twould be like him looking for a raven in a flock.'

'Perhaps you'll make your fortune there,' Ma continued, still stroking my hair, 'for it's said that in London the streets are paved with gold.'

'*Truly?*'

She shrugged and smiled. 'That's what they say. But it may be just a story.'

We talked more and decided between us that it was best for me to go; indeed it was the only thing, and I started to become more excited than fearful at such an adventure. London, we calculated, was no more than two or three hard days' walk away, for our village, Hazelgrove, is near to Hampton Court, where Queen Elizabeth has a great palace, and it's known that she frequently travels between there and her palace of Whitehall, in London. (She, mind, travels mostly by river, so does not have to bear the mud, the potholes and the highwaymen on the roads as others do.)

Ma helped me get my few things together – my second-best bodice and skirt, two undersmocks, some old silk stockings, much darned, which had belonged to one of my sisters, and my cloak – and, to go with my lavender-wand money, she also gave me a silver shilling, which she'd been keeping hidden from Father. I folded the garments as small as possible and put them into my basket together with handkerchiefs, washcloth and comb, and Ma put in some bread, cheese and a flask of water.

Our parting was very tearful, for Ma looked so old and careworn that I could not help but think to myself that I'd never see her again, or that if I did she'd be in her coffin. I believe she had as many concerns about *me* because she bade me to take great care where I laid my head, and not to trust anyone until they proved themselves, and especially not to be taken in by a handsome face or a hard-luck story.

'Guard your money well,' she went on, 'and always be alert for tricksters and thieves, for folk can get so desperate that they'd sell their souls – and yours, too – if they thought they'd profit from it. Remember your station in life and try to curb your curiosity, Lucy. Some things are not for the likes of us to know.'

I promised her that I'd remember all that and also that I'd endeavour to get word to her of how I fared, and, after exchanging many hugs and kisses, left my home for ever, so that my last glimpse was of Ma, standing in the doorway, alternately waving her kerchief at me, then dabbing her eyes with it. As for me, I was weeping plentifully and didn't care who saw me (although not being so careless that I omitted to keep a wary eye out for my father).

* * *

Within an hour, I'd reached the Thames, where there was a path of sorts, and Hazelgrove was a good distance behind me. I'd dried my tears and my head was already full of dreams of doing well for myself in London, of sending money home to Ma and of even, one day, being married and able to provide a safe home for her so that she could leave Father and come and live with me.

I knew I'd have to find a job straightaway so that I could support myself in the city, for the authorities were hard on beggars who traipsed the streets without means and would throw them in gaol for a spell, then drag them back to their own parishes behind a cart. This, I vowed, would not happen to me, for I'd begin searching for a job as soon as I arrived in the city and wouldn't flinch at any means of making my own living, no matter how lowly. Indeed, just the thought of being out of reach of my father's temper and his hard right hand was enough to make me feel very cheerful.

After another three hours of walking, however, I did not feel quite so merry, for my cloth shoes had nearly worn away at the bottom and, the river pathway being stony and unkept, there were now several cuts on my soles and a blister as big as a penny under my heel.

After examining these injuries, I walked inland from the river for a while, enjoying the grass under my feet and looking for some bruisewort to crush and put on the blister. But I couldn't find any grassy herbs at all, for the land was quite bare and scrubby, so I sat down at the side of the path and began to eat my bread and cheese, looking at the sun and trying to judge the hour. It was, I thought, about four in the afternoon, so I had perhaps three hours of walking left before it started to become dark. I certainly didn't want to walk that long, though, for I was hot and tired and my feet were very sore.

I suddenly realised I was sitting at a crossing of lanes where, it's said, they bury witches, so I jumped up and retraced my steps back to the river. I had to stay close to the Thames, for it was my guide; a shining grey ribbon leading towards London and my future.

I'd walk on, I decided, but begin looking for a barn, hollow tree or welcoming hedge where I could take shelter for the night. When I set off again, however, I'd scarce done a half-mile before I began to pass fishermen on the riverbanks and ferry boats plying their trade across the river, and knew I must be nearing a town. Sure enough, within another turn of the Thames, I passed a farm with a large flock of sheep grazing, then heard the tinkling and singing of weather vanes as a great building came into view. This, I knew at once, was the palace of Richmond, for some years back my brother and his friends had taken me on a rowing boat upstream from home, and that noble building with its chimneys stretching and twisting into the sky was a view I'd never forgotten.

The royal orchard entered my sight first, picked bare of its apples and medlars, then a chapel, set back;

after that stables, a brewery and two rows of little cottages. Following these came the great palace itself, several storeys high and topped by golden cupolas, shiny turrets whereon flags fluttered and melodious, spinning weather vanes.

Walking alongside high walls I glimpsed through gateways an ice house and an aviary, then a fine formal garden with clipped hedges in the shape of lovers' knots, shiny balls of holly and shaped box and myrtle. I'd have liked to linger there longer in case the queen herself appeared at a window or took a stroll along the gravelled pathways, but one of the uniformed palace guards appeared and shouted at me to move on.

As the gardens of the palace gradually gave way to pigsties and stables, then rows of vegetables and fruit bushes, I began to look for somewhere to shelter overnight. I was passing dwellings aplenty along the bank but they were large and imposing, perhaps belonging to the queen's ministers, and I felt far too humble to knock and ask if I might sleep in one of their outhouses. Occasionally I investigated a likely looking bush, but these turned out to be either too low, too scratchy – or one smelled so foul that I felt a tramp must have already used it as his privy.

Leaving Richmond, the river curved and straightened by turn as it reflected the sinking sun, and in another mile or so a church appeared in the distance with a range of low dwellings beside it. A few children were playing on the foreshore here and as I got closer I saw that they were a boy and two girls, all exceeding muddy and with faces as black as a moor's, taking it in turns to slide down the riverbank. The tide was out and the water was low, but from the eddies and whirls at its centre I could see that it was coming in quickly.

As I passed above the little group I heard a strange, excited chattering which was *not* a child, and I looked down and saw that the taller girl had a monkey sitting on her shoulders. I paused, fascinated by the tiny features and pretty head of the creature. I'd seen a monkey before, for Lady Ashe had one which she paraded around the village and which had its own nursemaid. She'd had hers, it was said, since her time at Court, and it had been given to her by the queen as a wedding present.

I knew that these children, then, must be from a wealthy family to afford such a pet. But if so, why – when it was almost dark – were they playing on the riverside, unaccompanied by nursemaids, and rolling in the mud like tinkers' children?

Shrugging to myself, I moved on, heading for some barns I could see ahead of me on the riverside. If these proved no good as a place to lay my head, I decided, then perhaps I'd have to turn back and use some of my precious money to take a room in the nearest tavern. But only if I really had to.

I'd not gone more than twenty yards further, however, before I heard a scream behind me and, turning, saw that the smallest girl, perhaps five years old, had skidded a little too far out and was now waist-deep in muddy water.

'I can't move!' she wailed to her two companions. 'Get me out!'

The other girl burst into tears and called that she dared not. The boy – who was only about seven – tried to move towards the younger girl, but his legs quickly became fixed in the thick mud.

'Help! Oh, help us!' the older girl shouted to me, and I dropped my basket and ran back towards them, picking up a sturdy branch on the way and then slipping and sliding down the riverbank, swearing to myself as my best skirt got covered in thick gobbets of mud.

Finding a secure place on the bank close to the child, I crouched down and pushed the branch towards her. 'Take the end!' I urged her. 'Take the end and I'll pull you out.'

She was weeping too hard to do so at first, and seemed not to understand what I was saying.

'Do as I say,' I shouted sternly, 'or you will surely drown!'

She reached for the branch and, as she clutched it, I moved backwards – but moved too fast, for she lost hold of it and fell back again, causing both her and the older girl to begin screaming anew. I persevered, instructing her to grasp the branch as tightly as she could and, as I began to pull her, to try and fling herself forward. 'You must try harder!' I shouted, as behind and all around us I could hear the water swirling and eddying, drawing up bubbles and gobbets from the oozing mud as the tide came in.

I pulled hard, she held on tightly, and there was a hollow sucking sound as her body came out of the hole and the mud closed up around it. I dragged her towards me, to the safer place where I was standing, and stood her upright.

'Does your mother always let you play in the river?' I asked both children rather sternly. 'Have you played this game before?'

The elder girl shook her head woefully and the monkey on her shoulder shook its head in imitation of her. 'They don't know we're here,' she said between sniffs.

'They'll know soon enough, then,' I said, looking first at the state they were in, and then at my own ruined clothes, 'for we look like mud-stricken boar-hogs.'

I lifted the younger one, who was still weeping, into my arms. The two girls were very alike, with small pointed noses, bright blue eyes and long, fair, curly hair which didn't look as if it had seen a comb for some time. 'I'd best take you home,' I said more kindly. 'What are your names?'

'I'm Elizabeth and always called Beth,' said the elder girl, 'and my sister is Merryl.'

I looked to the boy, but he'd managed to free his feet from the mud and was bolting up the bank as quick as a rabbit.

'He's just a boy from the village,' Beth said.

Holding the still-weeping Merryl, I made my way up the slippery riverbank. I trod with care, for the water behind us was coming up fast and I didn't want to fall over. 'Where is this place?' I asked Beth.

''Tis named Mortlake,' she said, taking a firm hold of my hand.

'And where do you live in this Mortlake?'

'In the dark house,' she replied as we reached the path at the top.

I was about to ask where that was, but I looked ahead and saw a forbidding-looking dwelling set along the riverbank which immediately answered that description. It had a thatched roof, which was heavily mossed, its walls were tarred against the weather with pitch, and it had tiny windows, which, though made of glass, were so dusty that they could hardly be seen through. I'd passed the house just moments before, but had not seen it, for dusk was falling and it had melted into the gloom to become part of the encroaching night.

'Is that it?' I pointed.

She nodded and I was amused to see the monkey do the same.

'Is anyone at home?' I asked, for the place seemed deserted.

'Mistress Midge,' said Beth vaguely. 'And our mother, too, although she is . . .'

I didn't catch the rest of her sentence, for I was

pushing open a creaking and ramshackle gate. This led into a gloomy outside passageway, whose only light came from a flickering candle standing in a tin sconce on the wall.

I shifted Merryl in my arms and began to walk towards a door which stood at the far end. It was then that I got the strangest feeling: a sense of foreboding, a shiver of fear and anticipation. Had I been to this place before? Had I walked up this very path some other time – or had I merely dreamed of doing so? Whatever the feeling was, I knew that this place was going to be of some special significance to me.

Chapter Three

The back door of the dark house was of heavy wood, curved at the top, with rusty iron hinges and a ring handle. Beth pushed this open and went into the room beyond and I followed her, not knowing and rather fearing what I might find.

It was merely a kitchen, however, as dimly lit as the passageway, with a wood-planked floor scattered with stale and ill-smelling rushes. A large table stood in the centre of the room and this was covered with piles of unwashed trenchers, bowls and pewter in such disarray that Ma would have been horrified to see, for she believed – and had certainly taught me and my sisters – that to keep a clean and orderly kitchen was a woman's most important duty in life. A huge cooking range dominated one side of the room, and above this were long wooden boards with all the articles of cooking upon them: saucepans, chafing dishes, skimmers, ladles, cauldrons and pipkins, all piled this way and that. In spite of all these utensils, however, and the vast array of copper moulds which hung on the opposite wall, there was precious little sign of any food being prepared; no enticing smells and nothing turning on the spit over the fire – which, anyway, looked to be nearly out.

'Where's your nurse?' I asked Beth. '*Have* you a nurse?'

She shrugged.

'Gone!' said Merryl.

I sat Merryl upon a stool and looked at both children, puzzled. This seemed to be a wealthy household, yet the children were strangely uncared for. 'Your mother, then. Where's your mother?'

For a while neither of them replied, and I wondered for a moment if I'd stumbled across a deserted house which had been abandoned by all apart from these two. Beth then said, 'I told you. She's lying-in.'

'She's just had a child?'

'Our brother,' said Merryl, and added very properly, 'he is my father's heir and his name is Arthur.'

'That's right,' Beth said. 'And he's *very* small and red.'

Suddenly the monkey took a leap from her shoulder and landed with a clatter on the wooden table, making several trenchers and two pewter mugs fall on to the floor and adding to the general chaos.

'But who's looking out for you?' I asked.

'Anyone,' Merryl said vaguely.

'Mistress Midge, our cook,' said Beth.

As she spoke I heard a-running on the stairs elsewhere in the house and a woman's voice scolding and muttering, as if someone was being chastised for a whole legion of sins. The voice drew closer, and then its owner came into the kitchen, stopped dead and screamed at the sight of us.

'Oh my Lord and Master!' said the woman. 'What is it but three creatures from the swamp?'

Merryl – who had stopped weeping some moments before – now began to giggle. 'No, it's just us,' she said. 'Me and Beth.'

'We were playing on the riverside . . .'

'And then I got stuck in the mud and couldn't get out and nearly drowned!'

'And our friend rescued us,' Beth finished.

Mistress Midge pulled out a stool from the ashes in the fireplace and sank on to it. She was a tall woman with a dishevelled look about her, grubby of dress and red of face – and stout, of course, for I've never seen a cook who wasn't as hearty as a hog. Her apron was stained, her cap ribbands frayed at the ends and her hair, grey and wiry, hung around her face. Her appearance well suited the state of the kitchen. 'My Lord, my Lord,' she said, wringing her hands as she looked the children up and down. 'However am I going to get you clean?'

'We must go in the tub and be washed!' Merryl said

joyfully. 'Set the water on the fire now!'

'But the tub has a hole in it,' said Beth.

Mistress Midge frowned. 'You must be washed in the big wine cooler, then,' she said, 'for you'll never get clean otherwise.'

'What about our friend,' Beth said. 'Must she go in the wine cooler too?'

The cook looked me up and down and tutted. 'I cannot see to her bathing as well as your own.'

I felt very indignant at hearing this, for I'd been waiting all this time to be noticed and even, perhaps, graciously thanked for rescuing the children. 'Excuse me,' I said. 'I know I present a shocking muddy aspect at the moment, but I'm in this state because I went into the river to rescue Merryl.'

'Hmm,' said Mistress Midge, pressing her lips together.

My indignation rose. 'Would you rather I had left her to drown? They were playing all alone down there with no one to mind them, and if I hadn't been walking past they would have come to grief.'

'That's right,' said Beth, and then she made a leap to scoop up the monkey, causing several trenchers and a copper bowl to fall to the floor. The monkey ran off, chattering, leaped on to the topmost board above the fireplace and threw down a ladle, which only just missed Mistress Midge's head.

'Lord, Lord above,' she said. 'That damned animal!'

Ignoring the monkey, I made an effort to brush at

my arms, which were caked with mud, lamenting the state of my apple-green skirts as I did so. 'I was perfectly respectable when I set out this morning,' I said in as haughty a voice as I could manage, 'but now I am all in disarray. I thought I might at least be due some thanks for saving . . .' I stopped of a sudden and gave a gasp, for I'd only just remembered that, intent on rescuing Merryl, I'd dropped my basket and hadn't thought to pick it up again.

Remembering this I straightaway ran out of the kitchen, down the long passageway and on to the river path, but it wasn't to be seen.

I burst into tears, unable to believe my stupidity in not keeping it within my sight. Sure enough, I had my money safe in my pocket, but what was now my only clothing was covered with mud and not fit to be seen. I had no shoes to speak of, and no smock, shawl nor even a kerchief to my name.

Mistress Midge, holding a candle, appeared at the back door. 'What is it?' she asked.

'My basket's gone!' I said. 'And my second-best skirt and bodice and some other possessions dear to me. I left them on the river path . . .'

'Oh my Lord,' said the cook, and she came outside, lifting her candle so that it illuminated a little of the pathway ahead of us. 'Some villainous puttock has made away with it,' she said, shaking her head, 'and will no doubt be presenting his sweetheart with a fine basket of stuffs this evening.'

I fought to hold back my tears. I'd only left home a few hours ago and already I'd lost the few things of any value that I'd ever owned. It did not bode well for my new life in London.

'Come back into the kitchen, dearie,' said Mistress Midge, her voice softening. 'I shouldn't have been so harsh with you. Indeed, I should have thanked you kindly for saving Merryl, but I've been that mithered these past days that I've hardly known my own name.'

I sighed and tried to look sympathetic, although could not help thinking that my own problems were more pressing.

'It's the mistress, you see,' she went on. 'What with her being so long in labour and calling for a little bit of tender meat and a nourishing caudle at every moment, what with the gathering of green rushes to strew the lying-in room, the midwives to prepare hot drinks for and the visitors calling to drink the health of the new arrival, I fair forgot my manners.'

I nodded and, having no kerchief to my name, dabbed at my nose with the only piece of my sleeve which was not muddy.

'The housekeeper left after a row with the master, and to cap it all, Jane the nursery maid disappeared with the footman,' Mistress Midge continued as we went back into the kitchen. 'I should have known; I kept coming across them whispering in corners and looking coy at each other, but could scarce believe it would come to that.'

'So the children have no nursemaid to mind them?'
I asked, and it was then, I believe, that I began to think
that there might be a place for me in this house.

She shook her head. 'It's always the way. Servants
won't stay here, you see.'

I was about to ask why this was, when Beth, having
poked at the fire, touched the grid of the hot coal
basket and screamed. The monkey screamed too and
Mistress Midge gave a cry of exasperation. 'You see,' she
said, ''tis all harum-scarum mad . . . 'tis too much for a
body.'

'Then why do you stay?'

'These babes,' she said, indicating the children. 'If I
left, who would mind them? Besides, I've looked out
for their mother since she was born – I couldn't aban-
don her. And where else might I be taken on at my age?
I'm too old to prink myself up for a hiring fair.'

I wanted to know more about the household, but a
plan had begun to form in my head. 'Shall I put some
water on to heat?' I asked. 'And then, perhaps, I could
stay and help you get the children clean.'

'You'll not get anything out of it!' she said straightaway. 'For this house isn't as rich as it was, and Master is
as mean as the Devil when it comes to the laying out of
money.'

'That's no matter.'

'And don't think that you can steal away with a
couple of silver porringers under your gown, for Master
has a big dog which will chase you down and –'

'Father does *not* have a big dog,' Beth corrected her.

'Hush, child!' said Mistress Midge.

'Or any dog at all,' put in Merryl. 'For Mother says they are nasty, smelly creatures.'

I hid a smile, hoping very much that I could stay there for the night at least, for I was fair exhausted and felt I hardly had the strength to go on further. 'I can assure you that I won't steal your possessions,' I said, and added mildly, 'even though it was through helping you that I lost my own.'

'Well, now . . .'

'But if I help you bathe the children, then maybe I can wash myself when they've finished with the water – and endeavour to clean my gown at the same time.'

'Oh, do let her,' Beth said. She appealed to her little sister, saying, 'We want her to stay, don't we?' But Merryl's eyelids had dropped and her head had slumped forward.

Mistress Midge shrugged and her lips twitched as, talking crossly to herself, she considered what to do. After a moment she reached up to take a cauldron from above the fire. 'You'd better take this, then – 'tis the largest,' she said to me, half-cross, half-resigned to the matter. 'There's a well in the courtyard; you can fill it there.' She raddled at the dying fire with a poker. 'I'll get the big wine cooler, and some logs from the shed to get the fire going . . . maybe between us we can get the children clean enough to say goodnight to their mother.'

41

'Is she in good health after her confinement?' I asked.

'Aye, she's come through the ordeal well enough – but 'twould set the poor creature back a seven-night to see the girls in the state they're in now.'

I took the cauldron from her. 'Perhaps, after the children are clean, I could sleep here in the kitchen. Just for one night!' I quickly assured her. ''Twill be too late to go elsewhere by then and I could sleep on a stool here by the fire. No one would find out.'

'Lord, oh Lord,' she said, shaking her head. 'I don't know. If Master discovered that I was putting up strangers and strays . . .'

'I'll be off straight in the morning before anyone sees me,' I said, and thinking it wisest not to hang around while she deliberated, I carried the cauldron to the door and asked where the courtyard was.

'Across the passage, through the green door on the left and along the corridor,' came the reply. 'You'll come upon it through the gate at the end. But wait!' she said as I reached the door. 'Go on your way swiftly, disregard any strange sounds and don't open any doors, for what goes on behind them does not concern servants. If the master should pass, mind you keep your head low.'

I stared at her. 'Who *is* the master here?'

She pursed her lips again as if she was not going to reveal this, then, after a moment, seemed to relent. 'I will tell you that, for where's the harm? 'Tis Dr John Dee.'

I looked at her curiously. 'I think I've heard that name.'

'Aye, you may have,' she nodded. 'He's a learned man who works for our good queen.'

'Works for our queen . . .' I repeated, awestruck. 'What does he do?'

She hesitated again. 'He's the queen's magician,' she said quite briskly. 'Now fetch the water and be quick about it.'

Chapter Four

'I may stay, then?' I asked Mistress Midge. 'I may stay just for tonight?'

'You've settled yourself into that space by the fire, so it looks as if you already are,' she said tartly. 'Besides, I could hardly turn you out of here naked as Eve, could I?'

I hugged a blanket around me. It was old, scratchy and like to be rich with fleas, but it would keep me from catching chill while my clothes dried on the line above the fire.

Mistress Midge and I had bathed the children and made them ready for bed, then she'd taken them upstairs in the house to say goodnight to their mother. While they were gone I'd washed my legs and arms as best I could in the tepid water, which was now a pale and sluggish brown, then sponged down the bodice and skirt I'd been wearing. When Mistress Midge came back we'd lugged the heavy wine cooler out to the river's edge, where we'd upturned it, then she'd poured me a small glass of beer, cut some chunks from a loaf of bread and we'd sat in front of the fire while she'd told me of some of her life and – when I was given time to speak – I'd told her mine. It was not, of course, as though I had much to tell, for, apart from going upriver to Richmond with my brother, I'd never been out of the parish where I was born. I had no sweetheart to boast about, had scarce any schooling and had taken no other work but glove-making and bird-scaring. How dull and country-mouse-like my story had sounded in the telling, especially compared to that of Mistress Midge's in the magician's house.

The dwelling in which we sat, she told me, was ancient and considerably larger than it appeared, consisting of about twenty rooms (she could not say how many exactly, as many were not used), and sprawled between the parish church and the river. In all this house, however, there were now but three staff: Mistress Dee's lady's maid, who thought herself very grand and hardly lowered herself to appear in the kitchens, a manservant, who lived out and attended on Dr Dee on occasions and Mistress Midge herself.

'At one time we also had a footman, a kitchen girl, a farrier to look after the horses, a nurserymaid, a pot boy and a dairymaid,' she said, counting them off on her fingers. 'But we've none of those now. I daresay the master'll get more servants at a hiring fair, but the next of those is not until the spring.' She sniffed. 'He hasn't the money to pay their wages, anyway.'

I was ready to offer myself for work and board, wages or no wages, but was a little apprehensive about what might go on within these walls. What was it, exactly, that magicians did? Some, I'd heard, charted the stars in the sky in order to judge others' fortunes, some concocted potions so they could live for ever, others conversed with spirits. Was it safe to be in the house of such a man?

'You said that servants wouldn't stay here because of the master,' I began.

She snorted with derision. 'Aye. They would see something strange or hear unfamiliar noises in the night and they'd be off. No staying power, these milk-livered lads and simpering lassies. They'd take fright at a sheep's baa.'

'Then does Dr Dee conjure spirits?' I asked in awe. 'Does he make gold from metal?'

'I don't believe he can make gold,' she said, spitting into the fire, 'or we'd see a little more vittles and have a few more servants around the house. And as for spirits and angels – well, some say he do conjure them, and some say he don't. What I say is, as long as he don't conjure one up in my bedroom, then he can do whatever he likes.'

I thought on her words and wondered what it would be like to work in such a household. I could manage the children well enough, and life here would certainly be more exciting than spending my days sewing gloves. In many ways, too, it would suit me well to stay here, twixt home and London, for Ma was not too far away and I might, on occasion, be able to go back and see her.

'I'm very good with little ones,' I said when Mistress Midge paused to take a breath from telling me of her trials and tribulations. 'I've often looked after my sisters' children.'

'Indeed,' she said, sopping bread into her beer and eating it with relish.

'I've always been considered very responsible.'

She nodded, mopping under her chin with a crust.

'For I've already saved Merryl's life!' I went on, warming to this. 'And I can work hard and diligently and do whatever I am bidden.'

There was a long silence. 'So you'd stay on, would you? And you'd not be scared by anything you might see?'

I wondered what manner of thing this might be, but felt intrigued rather than frightened. 'No, indeed I would not.'

'Very well,' she said then. 'If you're still here in the morning, I shall ask the mistress if you may be hired, for there's certainly too much work for a tired old body like mine.'

She found me a big old nightshirt of hers to wear, then went to her bed, leaving me alone in the kitchen. I'd promised her that I'd keep the fire alive and I got more logs from outside the door and, after dampening them so they'd burn more slowly, stacked up the grate. I then visited the privy in the courtyard (which was grandly appointed and must have dated from when the family had money, for it had a velvet seat and was studded all over with brass nails), pulled a stool close to the warmth of the fire and, resting my head against the chimney piece, tried to sleep. But of course I could not, for my head kept slipping down the wall. I missed my ma, too, and everything felt very strange and unfamiliar to me, for it was the first time I'd slept away from home.

Sleeping upright proving impossible, I found two wooden benches and fashioned a bed for myself by laying them together, placing the blanket on top and wrapping it around me. In this way, despite the strangeness of my situation, I managed to sleep for a short while.

I awoke suddenly some time later, though, and not remembering where I was, slid off the benches and on to the floor. I sat there quietly for a moment, wondering what it was that had woken me, then went to the kitchen door, opened it a fraction and heard, very faintly, a voice chanting as in a church and the light tinkling of some bells.

I'd not heard a bellman so had no way of knowing the hour, only knew that it was still dark, not yet dawn. Outside I could hear the river high up and close, lapping against the bank, so it must be high tide. Eight hours or so had gone by since I'd been down on the river bed with the children, so it was, perhaps, three o'clock in the morning.

The noise which had woken me must have marked the end of the ceremony, for in another moment all noise had ceased and everything fell to silence. I found, however, that I was no longer sleepy but instead filled with a great curiosity about my present surroundings. What happened in this house? What magick was accomplished within these ancient walls?

This curiosity, refusing to be quelled, fired up my senses so much that I knew I'd not sleep again. I therefore lit the scrap end of a candle in the fire and crept towards the kitchen door, for I had a mind to explore my surroundings.

This curiosity is a failing of mine, for since I've been a very little girl I've got into trouble by asking too many questions or doing what I shouldn't. I ate a black beetle once because I wanted to know how it tasted, and another time, much younger, I picked a red coal out of the fire because it was glowing so prettily and badly burned my hand. In spite of all these things, though, I'd always felt – and still do – that it's best to know the worst, and that if I was going to stay at this house then I ought to know a little of what went on within it.

Not that I wasn't terribly afraid of what I might find, and as I walked through the house the hand which held the candle shook so much that light flickered and juddered across the walls, and my stomach felt as it did when Father came home late from the tavern and lurched about looking for someone he could give a leathering to.

At the bottom of the corridor was the courtyard I'd been in earlier, and here I turned left and carried on further into the house, passing many more closed doors. Dusty tapestries lined the walls and portraits in ornate frames hung here and there. Lifting my candle in order to see their subjects better, I recognised our good Queen Elizabeth, and a portrait of her father, named Henry, who had six wives, and a line of other old people I took to be members of the family I now lodged with, for there was a strong similarity between the vivid blue eyes and pointed noses of these, and those of Beth and Merryl. The last of these portraits was a man looking to be about a hundred years old, with snowy white hair beneath a black skullcap. He had a long grey beard, which was forked at the ends, and he was wearing some sort of ceremonial robes, black and furred like a scholar's. He was standing beside a table, on which rested a brass-banded chest, and a sign on the outer frame showed his name. Though I couldn't read this, it was a short word and I recognised the letter D at the start, so was certain that it was my employer who was depicted. I stared at him, shivered, and walked on, and all the while the house was so deathly quiet about me that I began to think that I'd dreamed up the chanting and the tinkling of bells.

The flooring beneath my feet changed as I went further into the house, for it had been stamped-earth close to the kitchen, then it changed to herringbone brickwork, then to a fine mosaic patterned with stones which glittered in the candlelight. I went under an archway where the masonry was so badly cracked that shiny green ivy had crept through a gap and grown in a tangle across it, then through a hallway which was perhaps at the very front of the house, with an elaborate curving staircase leading upwards. After this came another passage, then a small and twisted staircase made of stone, then more doors. The house was such a size that our cottage in Hazelgrove would have fitted in thirty times over.

Reaching a dead end, I began to walk back, and just by the big, curved staircase noticed a large and important-looking door, enamelled black, with ornate fire torches to each side, both of these smoking as if they'd only recently been put out. After hesitating a moment, I put my ear to the door, but there was not a sound to be heard within. I cautiously pushed it open – I just could not help myself – and found the room beyond it in almost total darkness, with just one brand of wood glowing in the fireplace.

I stepped in and as my eyes got used to the dark saw that there were full heavy drapes at the windows and that the room was as big as a barn, so that the dim light thrown by my candle was not able to illuminate the far end. I could see across to the opposite wall, however, where there was a regular patterning which I took to be a wall painting, but on going closer found was shelves holding great numbers of books, *huge* numbers of books, more than I'd ever known or dreamed existed in the world, for we don't possess one at home, and the only one I'd ever seen before had been the Bible in church.

An owl hooted from somewhere, making me start, and I stood still and listened in fear, for one hoot is a sure harbinger of death. I heard two more, however, and relieved, moved back from the books, marvelling, hardly able to believe their extent. I bumped into a round table and, casting candlelight upon it, recognised a chest there as being the one in the portrait. Behind this table was another, larger one bearing many strange things: an instrument having glass tubes coming from it, a small cauldron, some wood and pewter boxes, an array of strangely shaped roots and pearly shells, half of a very large eggshell, a timepiece, and other strange and mysterious objects which I had no names for.

The Devil's work. These words came to my head, unbidden, and I couldn't tell why, for I'd hardly thought of the Devil before, nor what his work might be. I didn't like the room, though, for I was both apprehensive and fearful of the great numbers of books and all the words, knowledge and secrets these must contain. Secrets of which, being unable to read, I could know nothing.

The light from my candle suddenly caught something on the edge of the table, and looking closer I barely suppressed a scream, for it was a human skull, bone white and gleaming, its teeth bared in an idiot's smile, its eye sockets dark and hollowed.

There's something about the appearance of a human skull – perhaps knowing that it was once as alive as I am, but now is not – which drives fear into my heart, and I backed away from it in horror and left the room. Walking swiftly down the corridor towards the kitchen, I felt I had satisfied my curiosity quite enough for one night.

As I reached the ivy-clad archway, though, I heard a noise behind me, looked around and almost screamed to see the figure from the portrait standing there: the white-bearded man wearing a long cassock. He was not pursuing me, but staring after me with his candle aloft in one hand, as if he could not believe what he saw.

I began to murmur an apology for being about at that hour, but my candle guttered and went out, and I fled back to the kitchen as fast as I could, my smock and blanket billowing behind me.

I'd come face to face with Dr John Dee a little sooner than I'd expected, but was not going to stay and make my addresses to him.

I slept little after that for I could not help thinking about the man I'd seen and the skull on the table. Had Dr Dee killed a man, or was this an object he used for medical purposes? I told myself that it was more like to be the latter, for I well knew that moss scraped from a dead man's skull could be used in a cordial to ward off the plague, and there had been a bad bout of that the previous year.

Yes, I would think *that*: that he restored people to health, for I didn't wish to work for a murderer.

Chapter Five

'Will you stay, Lucy?' Beth asked, twining her small body around mine the following morning. 'Will you stay here and take care of us?'

'If your mama allows it,' I said, for in the clear light of morning and after a breakfast of toasted bread and warm milk I'd almost forgotten the eerie, book-lined room and the strange encounter with my employer. I gave a shudder as the monkey leaped from her shoulders on to mine. '*And* if you promise to keep this little creature away from me as much as possible!'

'Oh, don't you like Tom-fool?' Beth asked. 'How can you not? He's such a pretty thing.'

'I don't like him getting in my hair and tangling it,' I said with a shiver, as the monkey nibbled around my ear lobe, 'and I don't like the little droppings he makes everywhere.'

'Tom-fool is named after the queen's jester,' Beth said proudly, 'for they both make me laugh immensely.'

I looked at her, thinking that she was spinning some tale of make-believe. 'And when have *you* seen the queen's jester?'

'When Her Grace comes here with her courtiers.'

'The queen doesn't come here!' I said, for of course I didn't believe her. 'Not to this house.'

Beth nodded. 'She does. She comes to see Papa and consult with him about things. If we know she's coming, Merryl and I have to wear our best clothes and practise curtseying all morning in case she should address us, but some other times she comes without telling anyone and then we can just be ordinary.'

'Oh!' I said. '*Truly?*'

'Oh!' the monkey imitated me and gave a high shriek of laughter in my ear.

I gazed at Beth. I could scarce believe it, but as Dr Dee was the queen's magician it might possibly be true. If it was, I fervently hoped that Her Grace wouldn't come a-visiting until I'd obtained clean clothes and didn't feel so frowsy as I did just then, for looking at my skirts in the morning light I could see I'd not been able to remove much mud, but instead had just spread it over a greater area. There were half-moons of mud lodged under my fingernails, my pins had gone astray, leaving my hair all over my shoulders like a night-walker's, and my shoes were in tatters. I was in no way fit for a queen to set eyes upon.

Suddenly, Merryl burst into the kitchen, followed by Mistress Midge. 'Mama wants to see you!' she cried before she was halfway through the door.

The cook nodded. 'She does. I've told her all about you, and how you saved the children an' all, and she wants to thank you herself and look you over.' She winked at me. 'I think you'll do all right.' She bustled to the fire, poked at it, then put some milk on to heat. 'Madam *should* be taking the infant off to its wet nurse today, but now says she doesn't want to part with him. Him nine days old, too, and the nurse as clean and healthy a woman as ever drew breath!' She looked at me and rolled her eyes. 'The longer he stays means more work for me: napkins and swaddling to be washed, fresh milk from the ass four times a day, wine and little delicacies for the goodwives attending on Madam – and if the child doesn't go off to the wet nurse, Lordy, when will I see an end to it?'

I had no answer to this, and besides, Merryl and Beth were pulling at my hands and pleading that I should go and see their mother straightaway and secure my employment. This, of course, was pleasing to me and I was touched to find myself wanted by these little girls – so much so that any lingering doubts I'd had about working at the magician's house disappeared. I must keep myself to myself, that was all, and not go a-creeping round the house at night and taking fright at things.

'Wait,' I said to the girls. 'I must look respectable

before I go and see your mother. First you must remove this little beastie, and then I must try to put myself to rights.'

The animal being removed (causing some pain as its fingers were prised from my scalp) I scrubbed my hands, smoothed my hair and tied it back tightly with a length of cord, then asked Mistress Midge to make sure that my face was free of smuts and crumbs. Finally, I brushed down my skirts as best I could and covered them with a heavy linen apron.

The children led me down the corridor, through a thick blanket hung against the draughts and up a narrow staircase I hadn't noticed before. We then went down a long passageway, while I marvelled anew at the size of the house and tried to judge the number of rooms it contained. At length I was led into a fair-sized bedchamber which had clean rush mats on the floor and silk hangings on the walls. It contained a four-poster bed with embroidered drapes and, in view of the prevailing cleanliness, it was immediately clear to me that Mistress Midge's housekeeping duties didn't extend to this part of the house.

A woman lay prone within the bed with her eyes closed, while another stood to one side of it, rocking a carved wooden cradle.

'Here's Mama!' Merryl said, running over and flinging herself on to the bed, which was dressed very beautifully with a pale blue silk bed covering to match the drapes.

I curtseyed low before Mistress Dee, and then, on rising, looked at her with some surprise, for I was rather expecting that the mistress of this big house would be haughty and elegant; perhaps similar to Lady Ashe. Mistress Dee was not a bit elegant, however, and was not finely dressed at all, but wearing a creased nightgown (though 'twas frilled at the neck with old and expensive lace), with a faded dressing jacket about her shoulders. Her hair was caught back in a net and her face was thin and pale, her manner fretful.

'Lucy, is it not?' she asked.

'It is, if it please you,' I said, curtseying again, a little overawed in spite of how ordinary she seemed, for I'd not had an employer before and was not sure how to speak to one.

'It is I who should be greeting you with such civility, for I understand you saved my children yesterday.'

'Just Merryl,' I said. 'She got into some difficulties in the river mud.'

'I'm most grateful. But I understand you lost your clothes because of it?'

'I did. They were in a basket, which I put down for a moment and then forgot about, and that accounts for the sorry state of my appearance today, for which I'm heartily sorry.'

'Well, then. I shall ask my husband to scry for your clothes.'

I looked at her, mystified, for I had no idea what she meant.

'My husband can seek out lost things,' said Mistress Dee weakly, but with some pride to her voice. 'He's found a chest of treasure and several items of silver plate for neighbours, and he's also divined the where-abouts of a bag of coins that was lost.'

I gazed at her in wonder. He was a true magician, then. And if he could do those things, what other marvels could he perform?

'But until he finds your clothes you'll oblige me by taking one or two of my old gowns. I've asked Mistress Allen here –' she indicated the woman in dark blue – 'to seek you out something which fits.'

Mistress Allen looked me up and down for size. 'Why, she's as skinny as a pike staff,' she said rather sourly, and I got the impression that it was she who was normally the recipient of her mistress's old clothes and therefore didn't appreciate having to give them to me.

'I'm much obliged to you, Ma'am,' I said, bobbing another curtsey to Mistress Dee, then, to be on the safe side, one to Mistress Allen as well.

'And I'll be much obliged to *you* if you'd consider staying with us and looking after the children, Lucy, for Mistress Midge says you have a way with them.'

I nodded, smiling. 'Certainly I will, Ma'am.'

'My newborn, here, will go to his wet nurse soon, but Beth and Merryl need constant watching to prevent them getting into mischief.'

Both little girls fell to denying this, but their mother insisted it was true. 'They have been somewhat neglected

60

of late. At one time my husband had a tutor engaged to school them, but he hasn't been here for a twelvemonth or so. We'll have them tutored again sometime soon, and if you will be their nursemaid until then . . .'

I said I would and gladly. She said she had no idea of what wages I should receive, but would suggest to her husband that I got the same rate as Jane, the nursery maid who'd eloped, and I nodded eagerly at this.

She squeezed my hand warmly as she dismissed me, and the children then led me back to the kitchen, where Mistress Midge and I supped a small beer each and drank to my continued employment at the house.

I was given a room of my own – just a small space, hardly more than a cupboard – off the nursery, and told that I was expected to work under Mistress Midge and to care for the welfare of Beth and Merryl at all times. This sounded no great hardship to me, for I was out of range of my father and 'twould be very much nicer than sewing leather gloves every day till my eyes ached and my fingers bled. Besides, at home I'd only had a curtained space in my parents' chamber, so it was most pleasing for me to have my own room, which had a window made of real glass which overlooked St Mary's Church. It also had a bedstead with a straw mattress, some hanging pegs and two stools, one which held a ewer and basin, only very slightly chipped.

Later that day I stood in the kitchen watching the children play under the willow tree on the riverside while Mistress Midge prepared dinner. I was dressed by then in a dark brown bodice and skirt which had been presented to me by Mistress Allen and which fitted well enough, but which was very plain and sober without the least amount of tucking or embroidery. The other outfit was in dark grey and similarly sober. Mistress Midge said that the garments had probably been chosen on purpose, so that I shouldn't have anything too fine, for it wasn't seemly for a housemaid to wear bright colours, to have a large ruff at her neck or much in the way of fancy trimmings.

Now I knew that I was staying at the house I had many questions to ask of Mistress Midge and could not have had a better person to interrogate, for her tongue ran on wheels and the only difficulty was in getting her back to whatever subject one wanted information upon.

'Does the queen really come to visit here?' was my first eager query.

'She does indeed,' she answered, 'and she doesn't come alone, but sometimes brings her favourites from court. My, the Earl of Leicester is a comely man with a fine leg!' she added warmly.

'And who else comes with her?' I asked, but although she readily delivered a list of names and descriptions – some of the queen's ladies-in-waiting, the Earl of Somewhere, the Duke of This and the Countesses of That – I hadn't heard of any of them.

'Sir Francis Walsingham is a neighbour and sometime visitor here, and his wife is godmother to Beth and Merryl,' she said. 'Lady Walsingham – oh, a fairer woman I have scarce seen in forty years or more! And her dresses and jewellery almost outdo the queen's. Indeed, once Her Majesty told Lady Walsingham not to wear purple silk to court, for that was her prerogative alone.'

'And what is her husband?'

'Lord! Do you not even know that?' she said. 'Why, Sir Francis Walsingham is the queen's spymaster.'

I frowned at this, not knowing what a spymaster might be.

'Her Grace is beset with enemies,' Mistress Midge explained, seeing my puzzled face. 'That is, she has foes in France and Spain – the Catholic countries – where there are many who believe that she shouldn't hold the throne.'

I nodded, for of course I'd heard of this treacherous notion.

'So good Sir Francis has placed spies around the country in order to catch the plotters who would remove her from power, to endeavour to seize them before they can act.'

'He's very powerful, then?'

'Lordy, yes,' said Mistress Midge. She glared at me. 'To think they seek to replace Her Grace with the Queen of Scotland!' she went on, and I shook my head disbelievingly, for it seemed very strange and alarming to me that anyone should interfere with kings and queens. I'd always been taught that they were chosen by God, He alone, and men were not to meddle in such matters.

Dismissing these weighty thoughts, for I was hungry, I looked into the pot simmering over the fire. Not seeing a rabbit or any meat there, however, and the liquid being strangely pale, I asked Mistress Midge what she was cooking.

She sniffed. 'We are reduced to vegetables for dinner,' she said, 'for the household is very needy. Why, Dr Dee has not paid his butcher in three months.'

I gazed around me in surprise. 'This house is so well stocked with costly things, though – with paintings and hangings and tapestries,' I said. 'Can't some of them be sold?'

She shook her head. 'That's not the way the nobility conduct themselves,' she said. 'There's no food because Dr Dee spends most of his money on books. He has more books than almost anyone in the world!'

But, my stomach rumbling, I didn't want to speak of books. 'But what vegetables are those in the pot?'

She threw a handful of herbs into the water. 'They are called potatoes,' she said, and thought me ignorant when I said I hadn't ever heard of such things. I was rather doubtful about eating them, for while they were cooking they didn't look at all appetising, but beaten up with cream and butter they tasted very well. We also had some radishes, sliced and eaten with a tiny amount of salt, which latter thing was another new experience for me and which gave a strange shiver to my tongue which I couldn't have described. As I cleared away, Mistress Midge said that we might not even have had these meagre amounts to eat, except that some of those who'd consulted Dr Dee recently had paid him in kind.

While we ate, finding space amid the trenchers and untidy mess upon the table, cook told us of meals she'd had at Mistress Dee's family home, for they were very rich and had, so it seemed, dined every day on herb-crusted capons, soused larks, roast quails, fried salmon, lobsters and prawns marinated in brandy. Even more delightful to hear of were the dainty foodstuffs that would follow: cream custards, crystallised fruits in spun-sugar nests, gooseberry syllabubs, rose-water creams and frosted violets.

'Oh, do stop!' I begged Mistress Midge after hearing of these delicacies. 'For you make me long to taste such elegant fare and I'm sure I never shall.'

She winked. 'Perhaps you will,' she said, 'for if our master pleases Her Grace and gives her what she wants, then we'll be dining on these very things every day of our lives.'

'What is it that Her Grace wants, then?' I asked, eager for any information about the queen.

But Mistress Midge turned away. 'That's not for the likes of you and me to enquire,' she said, for magick was one matter she would not speak of.

Chapter Six

'Lord above!' Mistress Midge shouted, throwing her apron up over her head. 'However am I supposed to run this house with no other servants? 'Tis more than an old body can stand! It's Mistress Midge this, Mistress Midge that from morn to night. And now, if you please, the master has taken a fancy to having a jug of posset and some sweet biscuits brought to him.'

'I'll take them in,' I offered.

'But there are no biscuits! There's no time to make biscuits and no sugar if there *were* time. There will be no biscuits of any sort made until he's paid the grocer's bill! Tell him that, will you?'

I looked at her uncertainly. How could I ever do such a thing?

'Oh, 'tis past all endurance!' Mistress Midge stamped across the kitchen, causing Beth, Merryl and Tom-fool to skitter out of her way, and lifted a trapdoor in the floor. She went down a dozen steps then came up, puffing with effort, holding a dusty, dark bottle. 'Make him the posset, and he'll have to be content with that!'

I took the bottle from her and the children and I exchanged a smile, for I was fast becoming used to cook's temper and hardly jumped at all when she shouted now.

I'd spent most of that morning – the third of my employ – scouring, cleaning and putting away the last of the trenchers and bowls which had been cluttering the table, and following this I'd scrubbed down the shelves, swept up the soiled rushes and generally tried to put the kitchen in better order. Mistress Midge, who was overworked but also somewhat lazy, I soon discovered was only too happy for me to do this. As I'd worked, the children had gone backwards and forwards bearing messages from members of the household, who would ring bells to summon them and then variously request food, hot water to wash, that a fire be lit against the sudden cold weather or (this for Mistress Dee) that a sleeping draught be prepared. Tradesmen and cryers also arrived at the kitchen door at frequent intervals, selling foodstuffs, demanding money for past services or offering to buy or sell pots and pans, and throughout all this Mistress Midge kept up a fruitful flow of words: scolding, complaining, shouting or berating everyone in turn. It was fortunate, perhaps, that we didn't also have to answer the door to those who came to consult with Dr Dee, for the cook told me that if someone wanted his services – needed a horoscope cast, had lost something valuable or required a talisman – then they'd tap on the long window in the library. If he was at home he'd usher them in.

Beth and Merryl, of course, were so used to Mistress Midge that they were unperturbed by her chiding and reprimands, and, despite the irregularity of the household, were good and obedient children. When they weren't conveying messages from one end of the house to the other, they walked solemnly around the place playing a game they called Queens and Courtiers, or sat with their horn books, practising their letters. They showed me how their names looked, and wrote mine for me, then insisted that I try writing it for myself, so that very soon I knew how to pen 'LUCY'.

'Get a tray! No, a silver one,' Mistress Midge instructed me. 'And two silver goblets. Warm a pottle of sweet cream with six egg yolks . . .' I hastened to find these things in the kitchen, '. . . set them a-warming on the fire. Stir continually!' she added, as I left the pot for a moment to add more wood to the fire. 'Throw in some cinnamon sticks and the bottle of claret and heat together with some . . . no! There's no sugar to add, so let that be an end of it.'

I lifted the pan and sniffed at the mixture, pleased with my attempt, for the mixture smelled appetising and had thickened well. 'Pour it into a jug, cover it and take it through to the library.'

I'd not heard this last word before. 'Take it where?'

'The library,' Merryl called. 'It's the place with lots of books.' I smiled at her gratefully. The room I'd found myself in that first night, then.

I'd not yet come face to face with Dr Dee, but if he challenged me I was ready prepared with a reason for being seen wandering that first night. I'd explain that, being new to the house and its noises, I'd heard something strange and had gone to investigate. I'd then beg his humble apology for being abroad like a felon in the dark, and all would be well.

I put a clean kerchief about my head, asked Beth to check over my appearance and, setting the jug and goblets on the tray, set off for the library. Reaching the black door I tapped lightly and pushed it open, then stopped on the threshold and nearly dropped the tray in horror, for floating in the air close to the ceiling were two great dragons; dragons with scaled skin, gaping jaws, monstrous teeth and clawed feet.

Had I the gentility to do so, I might have fainted, but instead I cowered backwards, whilst making sure that I kept the tray and its contents upright. I uttered some small sounds of distress, however, and the two gentlemen seated within the room cast me quick glances.

'Oh, 'tis just a new maid,' said the old white-bearded one I'd seen in the night. 'Come in, do.'

'There's nothing here to be affrighted of,' called the

other man, who was somewhat younger and with a short, neat beard. 'All these are merely part of Dr Dee's collection of rare species from around the world. And they –' he motioned with his hand up to the ceiling – 'are named ally-gators.'

At first I was too terrified to look again, but then, seeing as the two gentlemen seemed so unperplexed by the dragons – *ally-gators* – that they hadn't stopped studying the papers before them, I dared to glance up. What I saw alleviated my fears slightly, in that the creatures did not seem to be alive and floating in the air, but were dead and suspended from the ceiling by means of chains, fore and aft. In the darkness of the night their presence must have escaped me.

I carried the tray to the table and, my fears eased and my curiosity roused, could not stop marvelling at all that surrounded me, for considerably more of the room's contents were now revealed in the light. A large window at the far end of the room bore a majestic coat of arms in coloured glass, and amber, blue and green light filtered through this on to the floor. On the shelves and tables, books by the cartload jostled for space with roots, urns, corals and the many strange things – including the skull – I'd seen that first night. Indeed, there was so much for an inquisitive person to look at that I knew that my eyes must be as round as porringers.

'Pour out our drinks,' the younger man said rather sharply.

I hastily did so. 'Mistress Midge conveys her compliments and apologises for the fact that she doesn't have any biscuits to hand,' I said, bobbing a curtsey.

But I don't think either of the men heard me, for both were staring at the paper before them, which I could see bore various diagrams and figures as well as some writing. I'd just put down the jug and had turned to go when my attention was caught by a large and bulbous fish, quite still, enclosed in a glass tank and set in waving coral fronds. I gazed at it in wonder, for its scales shone with all colours of the rainbow and it was a thing of great beauty.

'I tell you that I drew up the pentacle and used the incantation exactly as written here,' Dr Dee was saying to the younger man, seemingly oblivious of my presence.

'And you are quite sure you were not asleep and dreaming?' came the reply, with some disbelief in the tone.

'Of course I was not. Do you doubt my word?'

'By no means,' came the reply. 'I merely think it strange that apparitions usually appear to me, and me alone.'

'I tell you that I saw the wraith as clear as day!' Dr Dee went on, his voice rising with excitement. 'She was clothed all in white samite, and had her hair about her shoulders like a virgin. She seemed about to speak to me, and then she clutched her hand to her breast and all at once the heavenly glow which seemed to surround her went out.'

'A miracle indeed!' said the younger man, somewhat briskly. 'But I am still at a loss to understand – if you spoke the necessary incantations in this room and within the pentacle, then why did the spirit appear to you in the passageway outside?'

Hearing these last words, I suddenly felt myself growing hot.

Dr Dee reached for his goblet and both men looked towards me. 'You may go,' he said.

I moved away quickly, then closed the door behind me and stood for some moments in the dark hall, my heart thumping. It was obvious to me what had happened: Dr Dee had seen me in the night and thought I was a spirit; someone he'd conjured from the dead!

Should I go back in there and tell him the truth? I hesitated, wondering what to do for the best, for he'd seemed so pleased to have seen the vision that he might be angry, perhaps even strike me, if I informed him that he'd only set eyes on his new maid. After I'd thought about the matter for a moment I went on my way, resolved to say no more about it.

'I take no interest in the master's magickings and neither should you,' Mistress Midge said, sniffing. We were preparing supper and I'd ventured to ask her about Dr Dee's work and the seeing of spirits. 'I've enough to do with the wants and needs of people who're alive, without bothering with the other sort.'

A shiver ran down my backbone. 'Is it *there*, then, that Dr Dee's interests lie?' I asked in a low voice. 'He seeks to raise people from the dead and speak with them?'

'Some say so.' Mistress Midge turned away and bent over the fire to baste a small duck given by someone whose horoscope Dr Dee had cast. The duck skin crackled and spat, giving off delicious aromas.

I sniffed the air. 'Will there be anything left of that for us to pick at tomorrow?'

'I doubt it,' she said, 'for that pribbling foot-licker, Kelly, eats with the master nearly every day and will certainly consume every morsel he can lay his hands on.'

'Kelly is the younger man who works with Dr Dee?'

She nodded. 'I don't know why he doesn't move in,' she said sourly, 'for he's here all day and every day a-writing of his charts and pretending to see this and that. The mistress cannot abide him!'

'So both gentlemen seek to speak with the dead?' I asked breathlessly.

Mistress Midge gave the duck a vigorous turn on its spit. 'It strikes me, my girl, that you ask far too many questions for a servant.'

I felt myself redden. 'You may be right,' I said. 'My ma always said I was far too curious.'

The two little girls were under the table, rolling a ball backwards and forwards along its length while Tom-fool ran between them. Suddenly Merryl spoke.

'They *do* speak with angels,' she said. 'There are two of them who come regularly. One is one called Madimi and the other, Celeste. They tell Papa secrets.'

'And how does Papa see these angels?' I asked, looking eagerly under the table.

'They are viewed in a crystal called a show-stone,' the child answered.

Mistress Midge banged a trencher of bread down on the table. 'Enough! 'Tis not for us to know such things!' she said, and Tom-fool shrieked with laughter, as if he understood her words.

'It isn't Papa who sees and hears them,' Merryl went on nonetheless, 'but Mr Kelly, and then he tells Papa what they've said.'

'They are trying to get the angels to appear to both of them, to tell them how to do certain special things,' put in Beth. 'Like how to make gold.'

'They'd be better off making groats with the queen's head on,' Mistress Midge snorted, 'then we could pay our debts and have a roast duck each!'

Chapter Seven

W ithin a few weeks I'd settled quite happily
into the Dee household and it felt as if I'd
been there much longer. I missed my ma,
but Mistress Midge – scold that she was – in some
ways filled that role. I missed my father too and was
more than happy to do so, for it meant I also missed
going hungry because he'd drunk all we'd earned from
our glove-making, and missed feeling his clenched
hand fall with a heavy thump on to my head.

I felt so at ease in the magician's house that I'd even
stopped being frightened of going into the library. The
strange objects no longer scared me and as neither the
room nor its contents were held in any kind of rever-
ence by the children, we would play there almost as
happily as if on the riverbank. As for the books, well,
once Beth had taken down some of the great volumes
and showed me they were just letters within words

which worked together to make up a story, I stopped being afraid of them, too. I even started to think that it might be a fine thing to know how to read, for then all the knowledge in the world was available to you and whatever you were curious about could be discovered. Sometimes when Dr Dee was out, I'd slip into the library for a moment and just stare around me, gently touch the shells, corals, vases or strange roots on the shelves and approach the skull to try and overcome my fears of it.

One item that specially intrigued me in the room was the brass-banded chest, for it was beautifully made and seemed costly, as if it was like to contain something of great import. The padlock was always closed upon it, however, and there was no sign of a key, so I could only imagine what was within. Treasure, perhaps? Strands of pearls, sparkling stones and shiny gold coins? But then surely it couldn't contain such things, or the household wouldn't remain so poor.

Whether Dr Dee and Mr Kelly were true magicians, I had yet to discover. I'd received a message from Mistress Dee to say that the doctor had asked a spirit about my stolen clothes and had been informed by this ethereal being that they'd been taken to London and sold at a street market there, but I had no way of knowing if this was correct.

Sometimes, when Mr Kelly was in attendance or Dr Dee was casting a chart for someone, the children were given a warning not to interrupt and the door was locked against them. Standing outside the door at these times, I'd oft hear a strange chanting similar to that which I'd heard on my first night there. Once, finding the door had not been fully closed, I looked through the gap and saw Mr Kelly kneeling on the floor with Dr Dee standing beside him, holding a parchment. Both gentlemen were turned away from me and Mr Kelly was saying, 'I see her! I see Madimi. She's speaking . . . she is telling you to beware of being abroad on the fifteenth of the month, for it's an evil day.'

'Indeed!' Dr Dee said, and he appeared to write this down.

'And now she seems to be holding something out to you.'

'What is it?' Dr Dee asked him eagerly.

'A gemstone. One ruby, crimson as a berry. She tells me that she'll soon have the means to deliver it to your hand.'

'Is it large?'

'Very large! And it glows from within! It's worth a great deal of money – I can tell that from the size.'

I put my eye to the crack in the door (which, I confess, was very low conduct indeed), and stared intensely at where Mr Kelly was staring, but couldn't see or hear anything at all.

One day the children and I had the whole afternoon to ourselves, for Dr Dee and his wife, together with Mistress Allen, had gone to Richmond to take the new child, being now near two months old, to its wet nurse. A carriage had been hired for this purpose, and this had two horses in front like a cart but was somewhat grander, with seats at the back for four persons and a waterproof covering against the weather. We'd seen them off (Mistress Dee weeping a waterfall of tears at the thought of being parted from her beloved child) and then, with Mistress Midge happily occupied chatting with a neighbour, the children and I had begun a game of hide-and-seek about the house.

There could be no dwelling ever built which could better the magician's house for such a game, and although, of course, Tom-fool didn't understand (staying hushed while we hid, but often becoming wildly excited and giving away the whereabouts of whoever he was hiding with as soon as anyone entered the room), Beth, Merryl and I were happily occupied for more than two hours, using cupboards, empty rooms and dark corners to conceal ourselves in, wrapping ourselves in bed drapes, hiding under beds and tables, and climbing in and out of wooden chests.

Once, when it was my turn to hide, I left the children counting in the kitchen and hurried along to the library, for I had a mind to creep behind an old tapestry hung in an alcove on the wall and conceal myself there.

On entering the room, however, my attention was suddenly caught by the large stone fireplace in the centre of the facing wall. This, as far as I knew, was never used, for it had been superseded by two smaller fireplaces, one at each end of the room, these being thought to warm the room more efficiently.

Why did it suddenly come to my attention? I wondered this after, thinking it might have been the noble sculpted columns to each side or the pretty carvings in the limestone, but then perhaps it was neither, but just the spirit of inquisitiveness which has dogged me all my life.

As I stood admiring it, something made me wonder if I could stand within the fireplace and glimpse the sky above. I took a step forwards, then looked around one of the marble columns into darkness and sensed, rather than saw, a large space there.

I took another step, to the right this time, and found myself in a small cramped area like a box room or tomb made of stone; a space in which anyone might be completely hidden from anyone else in the library. Here – there was just light enough to see these things – were some traces of habitation: a stool, several grimy candles with flints to light them by, also a plate, knife and small earthenware pitcher which seemed, from the sour smell, to have once held milk. And everything I touched had the dust of years upon it.

I sat down on the stool in the almost-darkness, smiling a little to myself, for I knew the girls would never find me here. After a moment, though, I wondered if it might be better to keep this secret to myself. My reasoning went thus: when I'd been living at home I'd oft wished for a way to conceal myself from my father, and perhaps at this house, too, such a private space might come in useful. Also – were I ever to be so bold – by hiding here in the fireplace I might discover what went on between Dr Dee and Mr Kelly when the door was locked.

Coming out and brushing myself down, I went to my original hiding place behind the tapestry and happily managed to stay hidden from the girls for fifteen minutes or so. Our game swiftly came to a conclusion, however, when the small party returned from the wet nurse, together with little Arthur, for Mistress Dee had been unable to bring herself to part with him. They climbed down from the carriage, rubbing their bones and bitterly complaining about the jolting they'd taken on the journey, and the mistress, looking fearful pale, was helped straight to bed by Mistress Allen.

'Mama is being silly,' Beth said as supper was prepared. 'Papa said so.'

'Did you and I both go to wet nurses?' Merryl asked her.

Beth nodded. 'Of course. And when you and I have children, they'll go, too.'

'Mine won't!' Merryl said, suddenly snatching Tom-fool from Beth. 'I'll keep mine with me.' And she ran off with the monkey chittering with fright at being taken so abruptly, while Beth ran after to retrieve him.

Mistress Midge set me chopping bones for a broth and, being in a good mood (for the neighbour had bought a bottle of claret with her and this was now standing empty beside the water trough), began telling me more tales of her early life when she'd worked for Mistress Dee's family, and how she'd come here to Mortlake with her mistress when she'd married Dr Dee ten years ago. She said that Mistress Dee was thirty years younger than her husband and was his third wife.

'And she is said to have married well by being matched with him,' she said, 'but I don't think so, for she's still young and pretty and he's just an old husk of a man that even *I* couldn't abide near me.'

'And how did his first two wives die?' I asked.

'In childbed,' came the reply, which I might have guessed and answered for myself.

'But my poor lady hasn't won herself any great marriage, for this house is a warren of poor rooms and – my, to think Her Grace herself comes here! – 'tis most incommodious, for 'tis full of rats from the river and unwholesome draughts. The old dowager – the master's mother – I swear died of an ague she got from breathing in the foul airs rising from the water.'

'What was old Mistress Dee like?' I asked.

'A harridan. She posted rules in the kitchen that I had to abide to, if you please. Told me how I should scour my pans and keep my kitchen neat! And she was of the old religion, too, and – though this was before my time – set up an altar and took Mass in the library even after our queen came to power.'

I looked at her in wonderment.

'Aye, she did,' Mistress Midge confirmed. 'And it's said that somewhere in the house is a priest's hidey-hole, so that he might be hidden away quickly if someone suspected that an illegal Mass was taking place.'

'Oh,' I said. So *that* was what my secret place had been: a priest's hideaway. And it didn't seem as if anyone knew it was there . . .

Chapter Eight

A few days later Mistress Midge gave me a sixpence (which I think was her own) and bade me go to the market to buy greenstuffs. Once, she told me, herbs and salads enough for the household's needs had grown in the courtyard, but this had been neglected of late and little grew there now but tangles of ryegrass and nettles.

Merryl and I went together, leaving Beth at home to help Mistress Midge prepare a salve for little Arthur. His bottom and back were covered all over with a rash, they said, and he'd cried all night, which made me exceeding glad I slept far away from him. On the way there Merryl told me that her papa had cast a chart for Arthur so that he could ascertain what his future was going to be according to the positions of the stars in the heavens at the moment he was born.

'Papa knows *many* things from looking at the stars,'

she said. 'Did you know that it was he who decided when the day of the queen's coronation should be?'

I confessed I hadn't known this.

'And according to what Papa found out from the various configurations of heavenly bodies –' she spoke with very learned words, like no other child I had ever known – 'Arthur will become a scryer and be able to converse with spirits, so soon Papa won't need Mr Kelly to do this.'

I nodded, thinking that Mistress Midge would be pleased to see the back of Mr Kelly, but also that it would surely be many more years before Arthur was ready to take up his responsibilities.

The market was held in a small square outside an ancient building which had once been the convent, when we'd had such things. It mostly consisted of farmers and goodwives selling their wares from planks raised up on logs or from wicker baskets, and was very busy and clamorous as they were all shouting the various merits of their wares at once. I bought what we needed: a rope of garlic, bunches of chives, sage and thyme, and then found a second-hand clothes stall where, with threepence of my own, I bought a white undersmock which tied at the neck with a lace band and could be worn under my two new gowns to liven them. I spent two more pence on cloth slippers, which I sorely needed, and then, moving to the next pitch, found myself by a basket containing lavender wands.

Here I was immediately transported back to my home; to sitting making my wands at the rickety table with Ma embroidering her gloves and the smell of lavender in the air all around us. Suddenly I missed her very much and my eyes filled with tears. I hoped she was well, and not unhappy without me . . .

Blinking these tears away, I picked up one of the wands to ask the price, and in doing so my eyes fell for the first time on the girl who was selling them, who was about my age but a little thinner and a little taller. The bodice she was wearing was of pale pink linen, rather faded, and it had a small darn on the shoulder. The skirt was full and of a brighter hue than the bodice, for it had not been washed so often, and under these things she wore a draw-neck smock with a line of cheap lace about the throat. I stared at her with rising indignation, for the reason I knew these clothes so intimately, was acquainted with each crease and darn, was because they were my own!

I gave a scream. 'My clothes!' I said. 'You are wearing my skirt and bodice, Miss! *And* my undersmock.' I looked past her to her lavender wands, and noticed that the basket which held them was also mine. 'You have my basket, too – and my comb and stockings, no doubt!'

The girl paled and looked at me in fright.

'You thief! How dare you wear them so brazenly!'

Merryl, who had been wandering about the stalls, came back and surveyed us, wide-eyed. 'Are those your

85

clothes, Lucy?' she asked. 'The ones you lost at the river?'

'Yes, they are,' I said, most indignant.

A small crowd had gathered about us, seemingly glad of the interruption to their daily routine.

'Shall I fetch a constable?' one asked eagerly.

'Certainly, and at once,' I answered, 'for this girl is wearing my clothes and must be a thief.'

The girl burst out weeping. 'I didn't steal them! Please don't report me . . .'

'We'll let the law be the judge of that, Miss,' I said, speaking very high and mighty. 'I left this very basket containing, amongst other things, my skirt and bodice – the ones you're wearing now – on the riverbank, and someone stole it. Are you saying you're not the thief?'

'It wasn't me, I swear it!' she cried. 'Please don't call a constable, or I'll be put in jail.'

'But how did you come by what you're wearing?' someone in the crowd asked.

'Did the faery folk bring them to you?' asked another, drawing some laughter.

'My . . . someone in my family found them. They were in a basket and there was no one around and they didn't know what to do with them.'

'But you must have known they belonged to someone,' I said. 'Why didn't you take them to the constable?'

'It seemed like – like a gift from heaven,' answered the girl. Her eyes suddenly fell on Merryl and she gasped. 'Is that the magician's child?' she asked.

I nodded. 'She is the child of Dr Dee, my employer. I left the basket of clothes near to his house on the river-bank at Mortlake, as well you know.'

But the girl had turned ashen-faced. 'Please! Don't let him enchant me. I'll give everything back to you. Take this now!' She pushed the basket still containing the lavender wands into my hand. 'Come with me and I'll give you everything that was yours. Only don't let a horrid spell be put upon me and my family.'

I stared at her in surprise. 'But I would not . . .'

She burst into fresh sobs and I became confused, which changed to a sudden pity for her so that I immediately forgave her. 'Stop weeping,' I said. 'Look, I'll come to your home with you and you can give me what is mine and let that be the end to it.'

'Truly?' She clutched my sleeve. 'And you won't tell the magician?'

'I won't tell anyone,' I said, thinking that she probably had little to be afeared of, for the magician's skills were such that he'd reported my clothes to be on a market stall in London when they'd been but a half-mile away from the house.

We waved off the disappointed spectators and Merryl and I went with the girl to her home – a small, rough-built cottage a short way off in a hamlet named Barn Elms – and waited outside while she changed out of my clothes. It appeared to be but a poor dwelling, for I looked through the shutters and there was little in there in the way of furniture and not even a proper chimney, only a hole in the centre of the room to let the smoke out. The girl climbed a ladder to the loft and when she reappeared she was wearing an almost-threadbare skirt and jacket. She handed me the basket containing my other things, and all the time making so many humble apologies that I had to ask her to stop. We began to walk back towards the market together, for she still had six or so lavender wands to sell, which she now carried in a loose shawl hung over her shoulder.

'I made wands when I lived at home, too,' I said. ''Tis a nice occupation, but one that doesn't last for long in the year.'

'What do you do now?' she asked shyly.

'I'm nursemaid for the children of Dr Dee,' I said, and noticed the way her eyes looked at me fearfully when I said his name. I lowered my voice, although Merryl was some distance off, skipping along with Mistress Midge's basket. 'And so far I've had no reason to fear him.'

'Then forgive me speaking thus, but it's said that he's a necromancer – one who can raise the dead. And a woman around here swears that he enchanted her cow so that it gave poisoned milk.'

I shook my head. 'I can't ever think he did such a thing, for he's the queen's magician and surely has more important things to do than meddle with cows and poison their milk. It's said that magicians change metal into gold, but there's precious little evidence of that, either, for there is never any money to be had in the household.'

'My mother said that she had heard he speaks with . . . speaks with . . .' she seemed to find difficulty in saying the next words, and tried several times before managing, '. . . the *Devil*.'

''Tis not true,' I said stoutly, though a shiver of horror ran down my spine, and I prayed that I wasn't employed in a house so corrupt.

The girl and I exchanged names, and hers was Isabelle, which I thought very pretty, and we began to speak of lots of different things, for her life had not been so very different to mine – although she still lived at home and was the oldest of six brothers and sisters, while I was the youngest of mine. At each pause in our conversation, however, she'd thank me again for not giving her over to the Watch, until at the end I had to become stern and say that she was not to mention it ever again or I would certainly take her straight round to the jail myself, and we both laughed at this and became friends.

On crossing the common land we were about to part and go our separate ways when a band of youths raced past us, all wearing the blue cloaks and plain flat caps of apprentices. They shouted and whooped as they ran, and some other folk stopped them to ask what they were doing, and then ran with them.

'What is it?' I asked. 'A fire?'

Isabelle shook her head. "'Tis the queen coming from Whitehall in her barge. The 'prentices have run from upriver and cut across the land in order to see her again.'

I immediately grew excited. 'Is the river far from here?'

She shook her head, pointing. 'Just across the common.'

I called quickly to Merryl, asking her if she wanted to see the queen.

'I've oft seen her before,' she said, running up to me, but then must have seen the eagerness in my face. 'But I'll see her again if you wish.'

Isabelle had begun running across the common, taking a path over a stream and under the big oak trees. 'Make haste!' she called back to me, and I picked up my skirts and ran after her as fast as I could, crunching on the acorns that had fallen and dodging around the pigs that were feeding there.

We ran pell-mell towards the river and arrived in time to hear shots being fired, people blowing trumpets and sounding other musical instruments or clanging pan lids together and whistling. There were shouts of 'God save Her Grace!' and 'Long live the queen!' and, caught up in the excitement of it all, we too began shouting and cheering before we hardly knew what we were making such noise about.

We were only just in time to see the spectacle, for as we reached the bank of the river the queen's barge glided by, pulled by a strong rowing boat with eight pairs of oars. The barge was a beautiful thing, ornamented with paintings and gilding, having a cabin at the front with glass windows and a canopy of shimmering silk over. Seated before the cabin, raised on a golden throne, sat the woman I had long dreamed of seeing: Her Grace, Queen Elizabeth of England, waving to each side of the river by turn (for on the opposite bank, at Chiswyck, a like crowd had assembled), acknowledging with smiles and nods the tributes and acclaim of her citizens. Behind her came a flotilla of rowing boats filled with folk waving, cheering or banging drums; everyone there seeming to be filled with joy at being part of Her Majesty's progress.

As her barge passed, the bells of the church rang out, pealing again and again until this refrain was taken up by the next church further downriver – which was, I knew, St Mary's at Mortlake, next to the magician's house.

We cheered until she was out of sight, until we were almost hoarse, then Isabelle turned to me, smiling. 'She's back from a progress and will be going to Richmond Palace. They say it's her favourite.'

'Sometimes she calls on Papa on the way,' put in Merryl in a matter-of-fact way. 'If she's got time.'

'Truly?' I gasped.

She nodded. 'Sometimes she comes because she wants to find the best day to do something or to know if someone's love for her is genuine, and sometimes she has an ague and wants to know if it is like to turn worse.'

Isabelle looked at Merryl. 'Does she really come to your home?'

Merryl nodded.

''Tis true,' I said. 'They have told me so before.' I took Merryl's hand. 'We must go home with all haste!'

I bade goodbye to Isabelle, saying I'd certainly look for her in the market again. Merryl and I then hurried home, for if the queen was going to come a-calling, I had a mind to be there.

Chapter Nine

It was some few days later, however, that the queen called on Dr Dee, and I still wonder at the bravery (some might call it foolishness) which led me to do what I did. I was so very curious about her, though, so longed to see at close hand the magnificent and beloved person I'd heard so much about, that I scarce thought of the wisdom of what I was doing.

The first we heard of her coming to visit was a pounding on the door – the front door, that was – quite early one morning, and Mistress Midge being very put out that whoever was knocking didn't come around to the back like everyone else. 'Lord above! We don't have menservants or footmen, so it's left to the likes of you and me to attend the door,' she huffed. 'And I don't know how I can be expected to do it along with everything else, indeed I don't!'

I offered to go, for Merryl and Beth having not yet

emerged from their bedrooms, my nursemaid duties for the day had scarce begun.

'Whoever it is – tell them they'll be paid when Master says they'll be paid! And that they've got the cheek of the Devil to come lording it to the front door.'

But when I opened it, it wasn't the fishmonger, the draper or the butcher who was standing there demanding money, but a swarthy man holding a chestnut horse. He was dressed in fine livery of black plush velvet with a high ruff and lace at his cuffs, and in all looked so very grand that on seeing him I regret my mouth dropped open like that of a codfish.

Nodding at me briefly, he announced himself as equerry to the Queen of England. The *queen*, I thought, and, quite overcome, I thanked heaven that I was wearing my new undersmock and had combed my hair that morning, then sank into as deep a curtsey as if she was standing in front of me herself. When I rose from this, the equerry was still there, waiting, looking impassive.

From the kitchen Mistress Midge roared, 'Tell the boil-brained guttersnipe he'll have to wait for payment same as everyone else, and if he doesn't like it then may his fly-bitten backside take fire.'

Praying the equerry hadn't heard this, I curtseyed again, trying to gain time. Should I ask him in, or leave him on the doorstep, so I could go and find a member of the family? If he came in, where should he go? Was I to take him to the kitchen? And what, then, was to happen to the horse he held? *That* couldn't come to the kitchen . . .

Merryl rescued me, wandering up in bare feet, wearing a dressing jacket of her mother's, which trailed along the floor. 'Papa heard you coming,' she said to the man. 'He said to tell you that he awaits the queen's pleasure.'

The equerry nodded. 'Kindly tell your Dr Dee that Her Grace intends to visit him this morning.'

'I will,' Merryl said solemnly. She bobbed a curtsey and I did likewise, and then she closed the door.

I looked at her excitedly, ruffling her hair. 'The queen is coming!' I said. 'We must give you curls in your hair, put it back with pretty clips, make sure your new ruffs are ironed and get you dressed in your finest clothes.'

'If you wish,' she said with a yawn.

'Oh, *we'll* not see Gloriana,' Mistress Midge said. 'What do you think – that she'll come along to the kitchen here and sit by the fire with a pipkin of ale in her hand? No, she'll be consulting the master in his library.'

'But I *must* get a glimpse of her!' I exclaimed. 'Will she come on her own?'

Mistress Midge shook her head. 'She'll come with her lady-in-waiting – maybe two or three of them – her fool, perhaps, certainly some of her senior ministers and her food taster. She may even bring her personal physician, if she's feeling a bit out of sorts.'

'And where will they all go?' I asked, envisaging

them milling around in corridors, not finding enough stools to sit upon and being pounced upon and having their hair pulled by the monkey.

'What usually happens is that they are received in the library,' said the cook. 'We'll set two lots of chairs in there, and she and Dr Dee will sit at one end and speak in confidence, while her servants will be at the other.' She sniffed. 'Kelly will hear of it and turn up, no doubt! That beslubbering coxcomb won't allow Dr Dee to have Her Grace all to himself.'

'And will she eat here?'

She shook her head. 'Sometimes in the heat she takes a little cold Rhenish to drink, or on a dull day like today she may have mulled wine. Her taster will bring a flask of wine for that, though, for Her Grace's tastes are elevated and not like those of the common folk.'

I sighed, fascinated by all this information, and dwelling on this most amazing and astounding occurrence: that Queen Elizabeth, our reigning monarch, was actually going to be under the same roof as I was . . .

'Do you think she will ever marry?' I asked. 'Do you think it's too late for her to have an heir?'

Mistress Midge sniffed. 'She won't marry if she knows what's good for her.'

'How so?'

'Why should any woman content herself to be a tethered heifer?'

I smiled at this. 'But do you think she loves anyone?'

'Tush,' said Mistress Midge. 'If you're the queen, love doesn't come into it. If she has to marry then it will be for the good of the country.'

I gazed out of the kitchen window, wondering if there was any little thing I could do to make myself useful to her. There is a ballad, oft sung, of good Sir Walter Raleigh putting his best cloak over a puddle so that she wouldn't get her feet wet. Maybe I could do something like that, so that Her Grace would notice me and raise me. Maybe, then, she'd take me into Court and make me one of her attendants, as Lady Ashe had been.

After they'd breakfasted, the children were summoned upstairs to be with their mother, for it was hoped that the queen might wish to see Arthur and bless him with a gold coin. Mistress Midge and I went to the library and made up the fires, dusted the chairs and stools, swept up the old rushes and put down new. After this, I went to put on a fresh bodice and found myself spoilt for choice, for I was now the proud owner of four complete outfits, which could be matched each bodice with another skirt to make many more. Looking at them all, I only wished that Ma and my sisters could know of my good fortune, for being the youngest in the family, I'd always had to manage with their hand-me-downs and had never had more than two outfits to my name before.

After some consideration I wore my new under-smock with the green bodice and grey skirt, then washed my face and put my hair back with a ribband, allowing a few tendrils to escape around my face and curling these with my finger so that I didn't look too severe. I was anxious to look neat and comely, for even if I didn't come face to face with Her Grace I was bound to make some passing acquaintance with her serving men and women, those fortunate servants who lived at Court and saw her every day.

The royal knock on the door came while I was still in my room, before I'd had time to position myself at the window giving the best view. I knew that Dr Dee himself was going to usher in the queen, so I sped down the staircase as quickly as I could, hoping to hide around the corner of the corridor and see the royal party going into the library. I was a little too early, however, for they were still greeting each other in the doorway and I could hear calls of 'Your servant, Madam!', 'Your servant, Sir!' and so on.

The staircase on which I was standing almost faced the door of the library, which stood open and empty before me. Gazing on this door I suddenly thought of the secret space I'd discovered, the excellent place to hide, and in the space of a moment I was through the door, into the fireplace and settled in the hidey-hole before I could ponder whether or not this might be a wise move.

Once in there, heart thudding, I crouched on the

stool. Whatever had possessed me to do such a thing? It was surely *not* a wise move . . .

I didn't have time to change my mind, though, for almost immediately there were noises at the library door; the sound of feet rustling on the rushes, the swish of the ladies' immense farthingale skirts and the murmur of voices as people entered. And then the door closed behind them all.

I tried to turn myself to stone and make my breathing light and shallow. I was hardly more than a body's length away from the Queen of England! The thought terrified and excited me so much that I felt almost faint with the thrill of it.

There came some laughter. Someone – whether man or woman I couldn't tell – called in a strange, high voice, 'How now, Mistress!' and I heard light footsteps scampering, followed by the sound of applause. This continued for a moment or two and I took the opportunity to shift my body slightly, so that a slice of the outside room could be glimpsed through a crack where the limestone fireplace met the wall. But this glimpse hardly satisfied my curiosity, for I couldn't see the queen, just Dr Dee in his trailing black gown and another object – I didn't know what at first – rolling backwards and forwards, first out of my vision, then back into it. After further laughter and applause, however, I realised that the rolling figure must be the queen's jester, performing some sort of jollity.

When this movement ceased, Dr Dee moved to one side and was then joined by a woman wearing a dazzling gown of emerald green silk, decorated with jewels and ornamented with embroidery so lavish that I knew this must be the clothing of the queen, for I had never seen any fabric so splendid in all my life. I heard Dr Dee say, 'Would it please you to be seated, Your Grace?' and prickles of pleasure and excitement ran down my arms.

There came the sound of laughter, very light, and a voice – a queenly voice, for sure – saying, 'We will, Dr Dee, for we were out a-hawking in the park before breakfast this morning and our royal limbs are some-what weary.'

I heard movement and murmuring from the top end of the room, by the stained-glass window, but the queen and Dr Dee were seated lower down and, for-tunately, close to the fireplace where I was hidden. I couldn't see either of them entirely, but could hear most of what was said.

'Your wife has been brought to bed, we understand,' said the queen, her voice grave and well-modulated.

'She has, Your Grace.'

'And mother and child are well?'

'Indeed. They are in good health, if it please Your Grace.'

'Our congratulations. And so you have an heir, now?'

'Arthur,' Dr Dee confirmed. His voice rose eagerly,

'He was born on a most auspicious day, Your Grace, and I have cast his chart and found that he has the Moon in Sagittarius and many other houses in sage signs, which means that he will have great qualities as a magician and seer.'

'How extremely fortunate for you,' said the queen. There was a pause, then she said, 'And how go your experiments, Dr Dee?' Her voice lowered slightly, 'How close are you to finding the elixir? That *certain* elixir?'

Dr Dee cleared his throat. 'Rest assured that Mr Kelly and myself are diligently employing everything in our power to bring about the creation of this for Your Grace's pleasure.'

'Then continue apace,' said the queen, adding wryly, 'for we have already passed the first age of beauty.'

'Not so, Your Grace,' came the quick reply. 'May I say that Your Grace has an inner loveliness enough to put the full moon to shame.'

'Ah, good Dr Dee,' the queen said, and I heard a smile in her voice, 'if only all our subjects could see us through your eyes.' There was a pause. 'But there is another matter, and we have brought someone who needs your advice.'

How kind she sounded, I marvelled. How cultured, how gracious.

I think she must have turned and beckoned someone, for a moment later I heard, coming from the other end of the room, the heavy steps of a man wearing boots and stirrups.

'This is Sir Calum Vaizey, one of our most trusted ministers,' the queen said to Dr Dee. 'He has a particular desire to speak with you on a matter dear to his heart.'

Dr Dee rose and I saw the two men bow to each other, then the new man began speaking, often breaking off to dab his face or blow his nose. What I understood from his fractured speech, however, was that his daughter, a girl of eighteen who had been handmaid to the queen, had taken her own life.

'I am at fault,' he said, his voice gruff with emotion, 'for I would not let Alice choose her own sweetheart, but instead sought to marry her to a rich acquaintance. She said she would not, I insisted that she would, and soon after the wedding she . . . she . . .' His voice became choked and I could distinguish no more.

There was a short silence. 'Our children are a trial to us and a source of sorrow,' Dr Dee said piously.

'She died because I insisted on her marrying someone she despised,' said the man.

'But why do you seek my help?' Dr Dee asked. 'Is it for a draught to take away melancholy?'

'No,' the man choked. 'I yearn to see Alice again and ask her forgiveness.'

I heard this and, struck with horror, drew in my breath a little too sharply – then became alarmed in case someone had heard. There was a long pause in the conversation, during which I tried to steady both my breathing and my pounding heart.

'What you seek is forbidden,' said Dr Dee after a moment.

'But I know that you've raised spirits in the past. I've heard that you can speak with angels, so mayhap you can speak with my Alice.'

'But *this* . . .'

'I'm willing to pay twenty gold coins if I can speak to Alice again!'

I was startled enough to sit upright, wondering if I'd heard correctly.

Dr Dee made no reply.

'Thirty, then! Thirty gold coins for just two minutes with my daughter.'

My mouth was agape with wonder at this. *Thirty* gold coins. I could hardly envisage such a sum, or what might be purchased with it.

There was a long pause before Dr Dee asked, very low, 'Where is she buried?'

'She died when the Court was at Richmond. She's buried in the churchyard next to the royal chapel,' came the reply.

'In the *churchyard*?' Dr Dee enquired.

The other said, 'I had her death recorded as an accident to enable her to be buried close to the queen's apartments.'

'I will consult my charts and see if such a thing is

possible,' said Dr Dee after a further pause. 'I can make no promises.' He moved to a table and there came the scratching of a quill pen on parchment. He asked, 'What date did she die, sir?'

''Twas the fifteenth of September.'

'And what was the date of her birth?'

'The twenty-first of April.'

My heart gave a little jump at this, for it was my own birthday.

'I will contact you,' said Dr Dee. The two gentlemen bowed to each other and then came the jingling of spurs as he walked back to the far end of the room.

I don't think the queen had uttered a word all this time, but after the man retreated she said pleasantly to Dr Dee, 'May we set eyes on the contents of your box today?'

'Your Grace . . .' came the reply, and he crossed my line of vision once more and, I believe, went to the table on which rested the little chest. He then walked back to the queen and I heard a faint squeak as a key turned and an exclamation from the queen. 'Oh, such pretty things,' she said. 'And so potent in the right hands.'

How my curiosity burned! How I longed to see what it was that she was seeing. But I sat, utterly immobile, until she, after laughing a little and making small exclamations of delight, said, 'Thank you, Dr Dee,' and the chest was returned to the table.

* * *

Shortly after, the queen and her attendants left to go to the nearby Walsingham household. I never found out how many servants were with her that day, but I judged them to be about ten in number, and from the crack in the fireplace wall saw them leaving in a blur of brilliant-coloured silks and braiding, plumes of feathers, ornately decorated hats and starched white ruffs.

I listened to Dr Dee at the front door bidding them farewell – for they did not visit Mistress Dee in her chamber – and then, the room being perfectly quiet, judged it to be empty.

Gingerly, for I'd grown stiff and cold, I began to move out of the fireplace. I thought I'd attend the fire or do some other simple task which was an acceptable reason for being in there. I did not get this far, however, for the moment I peered around the fireplace I looked into the large and whiskered face of a cat. A human cat.

I think I screamed. I certainly gasped with fright and surprise.

'How now, Mistress?' it said, grasping my hand in a surprisingly strong, furred grip and pulling me close. 'I have been a-waiting for you.'

I didn't speak, for I was frightened out of my wits.

'And although I may only be a cat, I am tiger enough to kill a traitor!'

I would have cried out that I was certainly not a traitor but was unable to, for my assailant had backed

me hard against the wall and, staring at me with malev-
olence in his eyes, was gripping tightly around my neck
with both hands.

Chapter Ten

I was terribly frightened, for I knew well that the queen's person was considered sacred and that spying on her was a treasonable offence.

'Why were you concealed in the fireplace? Who do you work for? Tell me quickly and I can kill you all the sooner.'

'I . . . I . . .' I began, but I was, in fact, too frightened to say anything. Besides, his hands were still constricting my throat so that I could hardly draw breath.

'Speak, or this cat shall have your tongue,' he said. 'Yes, and your heart and entrails too, and they shall hang from the chimney of the house so that ravens may peck at them.'

I shuddered. The young man – for I could tell his age from his voice – was not tall for one of that sex, perhaps a little above my own height, but I knew from the sheer force of his grip that he was strong and well-muscled. He was wearing a black velvet doublet edged with white fur but I could see little of his hair or features, for the cat's mask covered most of his face, finishing under his nose with a flourish of whiskers.

'I have met your sort before,' he said, increasing the pressure on my throat. 'Prinked up to look like a maid, but with a dagger concealed in your bodice.'

I shook my head violently, indicating with my free hand that he was preventing me from speaking. He loosened his grip on me somewhat.

'Speak, then, and be quick about it, and let's get you off to the Tower without more ado.'

I rubbed at my throat, for it was paining me where his fingers had pressed into the flesh. 'I . . . I am no traitor,' I stammered. 'I merely wanted to set eyes on the queen. I have long admired her.'

He gave a short and scornful laugh. 'You admire her!' he said. 'I have heard many an excuse for being too close to Her Grace, but have not heard this before.'

His eyes were looking at me through the slits in the mask, weighing me up. They were not green like a cat's, but a silvery grey, and very cold.

'I swear I meant the queen no harm!'

'So said the last traitor who crossed her threshold.'

I swallowed painfully. 'B . . . but how can I prove to you that . . . ?'

'Enough of this! Speak now and tell me who is your master,' he said, 'or be taken away and have the truth pressed out of you.'

I felt tears of fear spring to my eyes. 'But how could I harm her – or anyone? I have no weapons concealed about me.'

His eyes flickered over me as if looking for places in which a dagger might be concealed, and came to rest at my neck. 'What is that tawdry gee-gaw you wear? Are you a member of some secret society?'

I shook my head. ''Tis just a groat. Not a real one, or my needs are such that I would have spent it, but a counterfeit.'

'And why would you wear such a shoddy thing?'

I flushed pink at the scorn in his voice, for I could tell that the cat's costume was a rich one, see that he wore a wide gold ring in his ear, that his doublet was edged with costly white ermine and his mask decorated with jewels.

'I wear it because it bears the queen's image,' I said simply.

'Does it? It also bears such a poor amount of silver that it has gone quite black.'

My hand touched the coin and I ran my fingers over the queen's profile. 'But I know that it shows the queen's face, and that is enough.'

He looked at me deeply, consideringly.

'I am no traitor!' I declared again. 'If you wish, you may search me.'

His eyes flickered over me again and after a moment his mouth curved upwards in a smile. 'Go to, Mistress,' he said. 'That will not be necessary.' He raised his eyebrows. 'Not this time.'

I blushed again, for I took his meaning. 'You believe me? You believe I am merely a housemaid and nothing more?'

He nodded and removed his hands from my throat. 'I do. For surely no one would wear such a tawdry object about her neck unless she was devoted to Her Grace.' He laughed. 'A cat may know a queen, but he also knows a maid.'

'I *am* a maid,' I said, nodding thankfully. 'I work for Dr Dee and am nurse to his children. My only wish in this life is to serve Her Grace. I'd never do anything to harm her!'

'I think you speak truly.'

'I do!'

'Then we shall be introduced. My name is Tomas.'

'And mine is Lucy,' I said, near light-headed with relief. I gasped then, and added, 'Of course! You are Tom-fool. The real Tom-fool.'

He shook his head. 'Not today. Today I am Tom-cat.' He took a step back from me and suddenly flipped himself over twice like a tumbling man at a fair, and I couldn't do anything but laugh and applaud, for he was deft and neat in his movements and very like a cat.

'Well tumbled, Sir!'

He bowed. 'Helter-skelter, hang sorrow, what can we be but merry?'

'What indeed!' I replied. I was certainly not able to turn a somersault, so instead I bobbed a low curtsey.

'But how did you know that I was behind the fireplace?'

'Where my queen goes, I go,' he answered. 'I have the sensibility of a cat and see and hear much that others do not. In short, pretty maidy, I heard you there.' He smiled at me again, and his grey eyes took on a warmth and a light. 'So, you would serve Her Grace, would you?'

I nodded fervently.

'Then you and I are bound to see each other again, and when we do it will be a happy meet.'

There was a short trumpet blast from outside.

'Her Grace departs,' he said, and he raised my hand to his mouth, kissed it and left the room, leaving me still quivering with a mix of fear and excitement. But mostly excitement.

I occupied myself by replacing the chairs and stools in their usual positions, thinking on all that I'd heard. And then, Dr Dee not returning to the room straightaway, I cast my eyes about it, thinking to myself how strange and wonderful it was that the Queen of England herself had been sitting there just a moment before. I wished I could have seen her complete, closer, in all her glory, so that I could have admired her jewels the better, seen how she'd dressed her hair, admired her hands – for they were said to be very slim and elegant.

It was then that I noticed something which made

my heart skip a beat: the little chest was without its padlock! I had not, it seemed, learned any lesson on the dangers of curiosity, for within a moment I'd swung the lid back on its hinges and was looking inside.

The chest was lined in dark blue velvet and contained two things: a small glass ball, about as big as a duck's egg but perfectly round, and a black and silver mirror. At first glance this seemed to be a looking glass on a handle, similar to the ones that great ladies have to apply their rouge, but when I nervously took it up I found that instead of one surface being reflective, back and front were both equally dark.

For what magick could this be used? I wondered. Pondering, alert for any sound from the hallway, I put it down and picked up the glass ball. This was of heavy crystal, a dead weight, beautiful, shining and clear; surely the show-stone which Merryl had spoken of? As I stared into it, entranced, looking deeper and deeper as if into a bottomless pool, I thought I saw blue colours within its depths: sapphire and purple stones, acqua and turquoise, sparkling altogether on a gold flask or bottle.

But how *could* I see such a thing? I looked around me. Was I merely seeing a reflection of something within this room?

But before I could pursue this question further I heard footsteps outside and immediately replacing the crystal within the chest, moved away to the other end of the room.

Mr Kelly came in, his gown and cloak askew, his face red with indignation.

'I've missed her, haven't I? I just saw her entourage going down the high street.' He frowned deeply at me, as if I was responsible for his not having been there. 'Couldn't someone have been sent to tell me she was coming? Couldn't you have come with a message?'

I murmured something but couldn't give a proper reply – for indeed it wasn't my place to make excuses on Dr Dee's behalf – and when that gentleman came in a moment later I made myself busy tending the fire at the far end of the room.

'Did she ask about the elixir?' Mr Kelly asked after some angry preamble, and Dr Dee murmured something in reply, two words that I didn't understand, using a strange language.

'But why didn't you contact me?' Mr Kelly asked again.

'I had no time to do so, Sir,' answered Dr Dee.

'But I am your partner. Your scryer. We work together, Dee. We work together or not at all.'

'Then hear this,' said Dr Dee, and he took up two chairs, placed them before one of the tables and, I believe, told Kelly about the queen's minister and his dead daughter. I knew this was so because, before leaving the room, I heard the words 'thirty gold pieces' spoken, once by Dr Dee and once, in awe, repeated by Mr Kelly.

I went back to the kitchen and resumed my duties,

thinking all the while about the two objects in the box, wondering if they were true articles of magick and, if so, what conjurations could be performed with them. I'd held them both in my right hand and I now felt an ache and tingle all the way up this arm, as if I'd been lying on it overnight. Soon, though, going about my daily duties, emptying slop buckets into the river and listening to Mistress Midge's complaints, I began to doubt my eyes. Had I really seen blue stones glittering within the crystal globe? Or, my mind half-expecting magick, had it just been my imagination?

The girls, not having seen the queen, came back to their room to change into their everyday clothes. I told them that I'd seen the real Tom-fool, although, of course, didn't tell them the circumstances.

'Oh!' Merryl said, sticking out her bottom lip in a pout. 'I wanted to see him. I like him! He told me that when I grow up he'd marry me.'

'Did he now?' I said, my mind still on the mysterious, magical objects. 'But I expect your father has a more prestigious match in mind than for you to marry the queen's jester.'

'But it would be such fun to be married to him and to help him dress up in different outfits all the time!'

'He's too old for you,' said her sister.

'And how old is that?' I asked.

'We're not sure,' said Beth.

'Is he handsome?' I asked lightly, which was a question of little consequence, but which could be explained by my being curious about someone who'd kissed my hand and called me pretty. 'For today he was disguised as a cat and I couldn't tell.'

'He is *remarkably* handsome,' said Merryl, 'or I wouldn't consider marrying him.'

'No, Merryl,' said Beth, 'we're not sure about that, either, for he nearly always has a mask on.'

'Yes, and when he hasn't, he's never still long enough for anyone to see him because he's jumping and rolling and turning somersaults,' Merryl said, and she attempted to turn a somersault herself, but only succeeded in getting caught up in her petticoats.

'But, Lucy, why do you want to know if he's hand-some?' Beth asked, frowning.

'Oh, I was just interested,' I said, and changed the conversation by bidding her to stand still so that I could pin her bodice on to her skirts without pricking her, a task completed successfully until Tom-fool the monkey spotted the pincushion, scooped it up and proceeded to bombard us with tiny darts, causing us to leave the room in haste and go downstairs.

That night, for some reason unable to sleep, I heard strange noises in the churchyard of St Mary's and, look-ing out of my window, saw by the light of the moon two shadowy figures standing over a flat-topped family tomb. I took these for newly risen wraiths at first and was set to scream out when one of them turned towards the house and I saw from his profile and lengthy beard that it was actually Dr Dee, with Mr Kelly beside him. I watched with an awful fascination as the two men stood over the tomb and raised their hands, all the time chanting a dirge, very low. I believe I saw the dark looking-glass mirror being raised in the air, and once Mr Kelly prostrated himself at full length on the stone. I came to the conclusion that they were in the graveyard for the purpose of practising their trade, and I say *practising*, for it couldn't have been Alice Vaizey they sought to raise that night, for her father had said she was buried in Richmond.

Such practices filled me with great fear, and did indeed seem to be the Devil's work, but I could not help but be horribly fascinated about the particulars of such a ceremony and want to know whether it would succeed. This time, with me watching behind my shutter, it did not, but my guess was that Dr Dee and his companion would continue practising, for thirty pieces of gold was great riches and beyond what an ordinary person would ever see in a whole lifetime. If Dr Dee was really without money, as Mistress Midge had said, then he'd surely go to any lengths in his efforts to raise young Mistress Vaizey from the dead.

That Sunday Mistress Midge and I attended church, going not because of any surge of religious feeling on our parts, but because an edict had recently come through that everyone in the country must attend church at least once on a Sunday or be fined sixpence.

The church was packed, therefore, but there were many stony faces and much muttering behind hands, for most folk didn't like being dictated to in this way. I, however, was of a different mind, for it gave me an opportunity to see other maidservants, to see how they were dressed and how they did their hair, to wear my best outfit – and also to see whether my employer suffered any distress at being in a House of God, for if he was in league with the Devil, then surely he wouldn't be at ease in such a place?

Mistress Midge and I filed in, found a seat in the church at the back amongst the servants of the other big Mortlake houses, and I shifted to one side slightly so that I had a good view of Dr Dee who, as befitted his status, was seated in one of the front pews. But to my slight disappointment, he seemed untroubled, and appeared to be singing in hearty voice, one hand on Beth's shoulder, the other on Merryl's.

After a long and tiresome service the servants came out of the church briskly – all the sooner to get home and prepare their family's dinners – while the well-to-do folk stayed to be greeted by the parson. I took this opportunity to walk across to the part of the graveyard which was overlooked by my bedroom window, where I located the flat-topped sepulchre where Dr Dee and Mr Kelly had been three nights before. This was a substantial family tomb and, though I couldn't read the names on it, I counted eight of these, two on each face of the structure. One name seemed to be newly carved, for it was considerably sharper and lighter than the others. I say I couldn't read them, but that is not quite true, for I was strangely thrilled to discover the name LUCY writ on one face, though this was older than the others and dark with lichen.

I didn't wish to draw attention to myself, so as I looked around I picked some herbs. If anyone asked I could say I was gathering rosemary to make a wash for my hair. As I studied the tomb (wondering if the final, newer name was the corpse they'd sought to raise) I noticed that it had a large symbol chalked on the top of it. There had been rain the night before, so this was not complete but seemed to be a large circle with a form of star – five-pointed – writ within it. There was some writing or sign at each point of the star, but these marks were obscure, although I could make out a crescent like the new moon, and saw also four short wavy lines.

I stared at these symbols, fascinated, then, seeing Dr Dee come out of the porch, turned away quickly to leave the churchyard by the side gate. Once back in the dark house I had all thoughts of magick and enchantment erased from my mind, for Mistress Midge intended to begin the big wash the next morning and there were soaps and lye to be prepared, and much shouting to be endured.

Chapter Eleven

On Monday night, I believe that Dr Dee and Mr Kelly tried again to raise spirits, for I heard strange sounds coming from the churchyard. I was so fatigued, however, having risen at three that morning to begin boiling water for the wash and then spending the day helping Mistress Midge scrub, soak, wash and scent the household linen, that I couldn't make myself stir from my bed.

The following morning, too, I had to be shaken awake by Beth and Merryl, but this was because I'd been woken in the middle of the night by a nightmare about my mother and had been so disturbed by it that I'd been unable to get back to sleep until dawn. In the dream I'd gone back to Hazelgrove but had been unable to find my old home, for in the place where it had once stood was now only rubble, sticks and stones. I'd searched everywhere, feeling that desperate panic of a child lost, but neither the house, nor Ma, were to be found. At last, though, I'd met Harriet Simon and she'd told me that my parents had been turned out of their cottage and sent to a house of correction, where Ma had died. Sobbing, I'd begged her to tell me that it wasn't true, but she'd just laughed – upon which I'd screamed out in my sleep and woken myself up.

All day the nightmare hung over me so that I thought little about my duties but much about home. These fears were further compounded by the knowledge that from early childhood I had, on occasion, dreamed of future events: about someone coming to the house and that person arriving the following day, about the weather turning and there later being a horrendous storm, or, once, a near-neighbour dying of an accident. After this latter thing had happened, I'd stopped telling people of my dreams and never attempted to recall them once awake, for I was too scared of dreaming that something bad would happen to my ma, or to my brothers or sisters. This time, though, I couldn't seem to shake the nightmare from my mind.

The afternoon when Mistress Midge and I were sitting mending the mistress's silk stockings I began to tell her about the dream, hoping that she'd give me some simple reassurance that it was nothing but a night-fright and that all at home was sure to be well. I hadn't got far into my retelling of it, however, before she stopped me, saying that she'd heard quite enough (for the stocking-mending had put her in a horrid mood), and had sufficient worries in the real world without being troubled by my mewling nightmares. I said no more, for I well knew that she had no time for talk of anything strange or inexplicable. It seemed that she could only work in the magician's house if she kept her mind on everyday events. Food, drink and gossip concerned her, but not much else.

My thoughts were all over the place that day, my fingers clumsy, so that I broke a porcelain plate in front of Dr Dee, spoilt a pottage by over-salting it and burned a batch of biscuits which the mistress had asked me to make. When Dr Dee sent for me that evening, therefore, I knew I'd been careless and thought he might be about to chastise me or even tell me that my services in the house were no longer required. As I made my way to see him in the library, therefore, I was practising my apologies.

I knocked and entered as usual, sank into a curtsey, and when I straightened up, I saw that Dr Dee had Mr Kelly with him. They were sitting one each side of the small table on which reposed the skull.

'Lucy, is it not?' asked Dr Dee. I had been in his presence perhaps five times by then, but he always looked at me with slight surprise, as if he was seeing me for the first time. I was so certain that he was going to say I must leave his house that my mouth dried up and I could only nod that yes, that was my name.

Instead of listing my failings as a maid, however, he

began, 'My children profess themselves very content to have you as their nurse.'

I managed to say, 'Thank you, Sir,' although I was still waiting for him to add, '*But...*'

The two gentlemen exchanged glances, then Mr Kelly, looking me up and down carefully, murmured, 'I have seen a miniature of the girl in question and yes, this one is quite like. With a little care...'

'Perhaps wearing a similar gown?'

'And at night, by the light of a candle, certainly...'

I looked from one to the other, having no idea of what they were speaking of and just relieved that it didn't seem I'd lost my position in the household. They asked me to take a couple of turns about the room so that they could judge how I walked, then just sat, murmuring together and nodding thoughtfully.

'Go on, Dee,' said Mr Kelly at last.

'Yes. Quite,' Dr Dee said. 'Lucy, I ... therefore ... that is, we ...' He hesitated and, placing his fingers on the skull, stroked the smooth round top of it with a caressing movement, as one might stroke a pet cat.

'Do get on with it, Dee,' put in Mr Kelly.

'Yes. Indeed.' He coughed. 'In fact, Lucy, there is a matter on which we think you might be of some not inconsiderable assistance.'

I looked at him, puzzled.

'It may seem very unusual to you, and you may not have heard before of such a proposition, but –'

'Child,' Mr Kelly interrupted impatiently, 'have you

122

ever seen a masquerade or dumb show?'

I nodded. 'They are acted in my home village on a fair day.'

'Quite,' said Mr Kelly. 'So that you know that a masquerade is merely when a figure – or group of figures – acts out a charade or a pantomime.'

I nodded again, wondering why I was being asked such things. 'They were performed by travelling players, acting on the back of carts.'

'And did you enjoy such pieces?' Dr Dee enquired.

'I did, Sir,' I said readily. 'For they were most excellent entertainment.'

There was a moment's silence, then Mr Kelly went on, 'Would you care to take part in such a performance?'

'To act on a cart, Sir?' I asked, mystified.

'Not on a cart,' said Dr Dee, 'but in a field. That is, something very like a field.'

'It will be in a churchyard,' put in Mr Kelly briskly. 'Let's be quite clear about that, Dee. We don't want her taking fright at the last moment.'

I stared from one to the other and suddenly realised what they were about to ask of me. They could not raise the daughter of Lord Vaizey from the dead, *so wanted me to pretend to be her*.

'I don't understand,' I said, to gain time. 'I've no experience of play-acting and could not learn words, for I can't read.'

Dr Dee whispered something to Mr Kelly, who frowned. 'Tell her straight what she'll have to do,' he said, 'for she must do it willingly or not at all. The scheme will fail if she's not committed to it.'

There was another silence, during which my eyes seemed to be drawn to that dread skull under Dr Dee's hand.

'All you have to do, Lucy,' said that gentleman at last, 'is to appear, dressed as a young woman of the aristocracy, and speak a few words.'

'Words we will teach you, which may be learned parrot-fashion,' interposed Mr Kelly.

I was forward enough to ask, 'And who will be my audience for this play-acting?'

''Twill be just one man and ourselves,' answered Dr Dee.

The dead girl's father, I thought. The man I'd heard speaking when I'd been hidden in the fireplace. 'It seems a very small audience for an entertainment,' I said boldly.

Mr Kelly affected a laugh. 'Oh, 'tis but a fancy someone has. An idle amusement for someone rich.'

I began shaking my head. 'I do beg your pardon, but I have always been told that 'tis not becoming for a woman to appear on a stage and play-act.'

''Tis not exactly a stage,' said Mr Kelly.

'And women appear in private masques – the church authorities have no objection to that. Why, even the queen goes masquerading,' said Dr Dee.

'No, I couldn't do it,' I said, shivering all over. 'You'll excuse me, but I truly could not.'

Mr Kelly tapped his pocket. 'Look to your purse,' he said. 'There's a gold angel in it for you.'

'More money than you've ever seen before, I warrant!'

It was, indeed, yet the thought of taking part in such a pretence was so frightening to me that I carried on shaking my head, all the while thinking of a way to refuse them without incurring their anger. 'I have a good reason for saying no,' I said finally.

'And what would that be?' Mr Kelly asked.

'My father is a Puritan,' I said (I lied, of course, for his only church is the ale house), 'and he's always been strict about such things. I couldn't go against all that I've been taught.'

'But you are not in your father's household now,' protested Mr Kelly.

'Come – we'll make it two angels,' said Dr Dee. 'Two gold coins just for you.'

But even for two angels I could not – would not – get involved in the deception, for I greatly feared the devilish practice of it, and also pitied the bereaved father, Lord Vaizey, and wanted no part in the misleading of him.

Begging their pardons heartily once again, I said that I relished working in the household and hoped that my refusal wouldn't go against me. I then went to my room to think on what I'd been asked to do and wonder on Dr Dee and Mr Kelly's competence as necromancers, for it seemed to me that they could not truly be capable of raising dead corpses, or would not have risked all by asking me to be a substitute.

The following day I went with Beth and Merryl to the market. Dr Dee must have obtained credit from somewhere – perhaps in anticipation of the thirty gold angels he hoped he had coming to him – for in my pocket was a list of things to buy and several silver shillings. As we walked, Beth and Merryl tested me on the items on the list, and I proudly read out the groceries they'd written down under Mistress Midge's dictation: *a rope of onions, twelve sausages, six red herrings, fine wheat flour, a sugar loaf, some cloves, mace and saffron.* I was fast learning to read, and hardly stumbled on any word apart from *onions*, which I found devilish difficult.

'And when we get home, you must try writing down the words yourself,' Beth said.

'And we will rap your knuckles if you don't get them right,' added Merryl.

Reaching the market place and looking around, I saw my new friend, Isabelle, selling squares of iced gingerbread from a tray. She looked pleased to see me, though went quite pink with embarrassment when Merryl said solemnly to Beth that she was the girl who'd stolen Lucy's basket of clothes. I hushed her, saying it wasn't Isabelle herself who'd stolen them, and anyway, it had just been a misunderstanding. Isabelle was, I noticed, wearing the same skirt and bodice that she'd changed into a week previously, and which now had a large rent down the front where the worn material had pulled away from a seam. This must be her only outfit, I thought, and rather pitied her.

'Has the queen come to call on you?' she asked eagerly.

'She has!' I replied, and though I wanted to tell her how I'd hidden, I was unable to do so with Merryl and Beth within earshot.

'We didn't see her,' said Merryl, 'for she just came to speak to Papa.'

'I *did* just glimpse her,' I said.

Isabelle's eyes lit up. 'And what was she wearing? How did she look? Did she have many jewels about her person?'

'It was just a tiny glance,' I admitted, 'and I saw only parts of her gown, but it was bejewelled all over and very fine.'

'I saw her once being carried on a litter,' responded Isabelle. 'She had a string of sapphires around her neck and each one was as big as a plum!'

We spoke some more of the queen and who she loved, for all the talk still, everywhere, was of whether she might marry and who would be the chosen man. When a woman stopped to buy gingerbread from Isabelle's tray, however, the girls and I went on to do our shopping, saying that we'd look for her later.

The shopping took some time, for there was a great deal of choice – much more so than in Hazelgrove –

and each item we bought had to be inspected, compared with another and bargained for before it was purchased. Mistress Midge, although lax on most things, was very concerned that we should always obtain value for money and I knew she'd examine our purchases carefully when we got home.

I only saw Isabelle once more, very briefly, and I asked her to come and visit me one afternoon, for – although I didn't tell her this – I had a mind to give her one of my old gowns.

'You want me to come to the magician's house?' she said, her eyes wide.

'It's quite safe, I assure you, and not at all frightening,' I said. 'Look at me and Beth and Merryl – there's nothing alarming about us, is there?'

She hesitated. 'It doesn't seem so . . .'

'Then come when you have time.'

She promised she would and I went home glad that I'd made a friend of her, for I longed to tell someone all that went on at the house, and inform her of what Dr Dee and Mr Kelly had asked me to do. I could never tell Mistress Midge, of course, for then I'd have to tell her that I'd found the priest's hideaway. Besides, I knew that she'd certainly have nothing to do with any talk of the raising of Mistress Vaizey.

It was two more days before Isabelle came to visit. It was afternoon and the girls had gone to take a nap when I heard the sound of hooves on the river path, followed by a tentative tap on the window. When I went out, Isabelle was standing there holding the reins of a fine, tall black horse, saddled in leather and with a red bridle and plaited tail.

'Is he yours?' I said in surprise, although I knew he couldn't possibly be.

She shook her head. 'My brothers are 'prentices in a livery yard and have horses to exercise every day. If there are too many, they send one for me to ride.'

I patted the horse's glossy flanks, then reached up to a tree to pick a crab apple to give to him. He took it between his teeth for a moment, then dropped it.

Isabelle laughed. 'He scorns those! He's a gent'man's horse and has been brought up on hot bran and honey. Do you ride?' she asked.

I shook my head. 'I've sat on a horse, but only play-riding. I've never used a saddle and stirrups.'

''Tis easy,' she said. 'The horse does all the work. Would you care to take a trot, sitting behind me?'

I nodded, eager for any sort of distraction from the afternoon's routines.

She looked at me shyly. 'Perhaps you could ask your housekeeper to excuse you for an hour or so and we can take a little canter in Richmond Park?'

I nodded and then my heart leaped, for it had occurred to me that we might visit the place which had been on my mind ever since my nightmare. 'How far can a horse travel in an afternoon?' I asked.

She shrugged. 'A good, healthy horse can be ridden

until he drops. This one could ride to London and back, for sure.'

'Oh, I shouldn't want to ride as far as that.'

'Then where do you wish to go?'

'To see my ma in my home village,' I said eagerly. 'Would we be able to go there, do you think?'

Isabelle nodded. 'I daresay . . . if you know the way.'

I pointed downriver with some excitement. ''Tis Hazelgrove. Along the riverbank and past Richmond.'

She smiled. 'Go and ask if you may absent yourself for a few hours, then, and fetch your cloak, and you and I shall have an adventure.'

Chapter Twelve

It took me a little time to get used to the movements of the horse, for I felt very unsteady mounted behind Isabella with no stirrups nor reins of my own to hold on to. She didn't keep both legs to the side, but rode like a man on a pillion saddle, with one leg each side of the horse. I travelled the same way, clasping her tightly around the waist, and once I'd learned to mimic her movements, to bounce up and down in rhythm just as she bounced, I began to feel more confident and was able to relax, and soon we fell to talking.

Isabelle first told me of her life, which was a sad one, for her father had died six years ago when plague had struck. At first the parish had provided for her family out of charity, but then, due to their extreme poverty, her ma had been forced to take work at a local rope-makers. Isabelle, then ten years old, had also gone out to work to help the family survive. 'One winter we were so poor we were reduced to eating turnips,' she told me, 'and as there was no fire to cook them on, we had them raw.'

I shuddered, for we had never been *that* poor.

'Of the five others, two were but babes when Pa died, so Ma and I had to tie them in their cots when we went out to work.' She sighed. 'They got up to all sorts of mischiefs.'

'And what sort of jobs do you do?'

'Any little matters in the houses of the gentry,' she replied. 'Repairing torn lace and ruffs, helping with the wash, cleaning out the sooty ranges or making soaps. Sometimes I'd work in a blacksmith's, holding the horses, or in the tavern washing pots. Now, though, I'm mostly at the market selling stuffs – whatever I can buy cheaply that day.' She half-turned to look at me, smiling. 'And sometimes I put on a sombre expression and a black hood and get myself hired for funeral processions.'

I laughed, surprised.

'Not many will do it,' she said, 'but 'tis worth a good deal, for as well as a silver coin, mourners always get given a new pair of leather gloves, black shoes and sometimes a cloak besides. And all we have to do is walk beside the corpse with a sombre face and shed a few tears. Once I was given an expensive piece of black lace to wear over my face which I sold after for sixpence.'

We approached Richmond and, the path beneath us

being sound, she took the horse into a canter. This made me rather afraid, for despite my new confidence it was a tall horse and the earth seemed a long way off.

'We can get by now, for everyone but little Margaret is out at work,' she continued, 'and next year she will be able to come with me to funerals, for she has a bonny, sad face and I've taught her to cry on command.'

'You've left out one of your jobs,' I said. 'For sometimes you make lavender wands.'

'Sometimes I do,' she said, and hesitated. 'There's something I must say on that . . . on the manner in which we met.'

'Please don't,' I said, fearing she was going to begin apologising once more.

'No, I must tell! It was one of my brothers, you see, who found your basket on the riverbank, and he brought it home to show us. Ma said we must take it to the constable and we were about to do so when I saw your bodice and skirt in there, and had a fancy to try them on – though I knew I shouldn't have done so, and that it was very wrong of me.'

She faltered and I squeezed her arm to say that I understood.

'And then, when I put them on they fitted me so perfectly with scarcely a tuck or a pin needed that even Ma said they must have been made for me, and my little brothers all said how comely I looked, and with my own gown being almost in tatters I decided . . .'

'It doesn't matter,' I said, smiling as I thought of what I was planning. 'My new mistress has seen that I'm fitted out and I now have four outfits all of my own!'

'She's kind to you, then?'

'She is, though she's still confined to bed and I rarely see her.'

'And what of your famed master. What of Dr Dee?'

'He is peculiar enough,' I said, eager to tell someone of my life with the Dee family, 'and the household is a strange one, for though 'tis rich in books and paintings – and the children have a monkey for a pet – until recently there has never been enough money to spend on things like food.'

'How so?'

'Well, because along with all the books he buys, Dr Dee collects strange things from other countries, *specimens*, and puts these things about his room, which is a library. Have you heard of an ally-gator?'

'Never. What is one?'

'A creature very like a dragon.'

'He has one in the house?' she said in alarm.

'Two,' I said. 'But they are dead and stuffed. And more strange things, too: giant eggs and great bird's nests, pearly shells as big as a man's hat and tiny little horse-like creatures that swim in a tank of water.'

She turned to look at me wonderingly. 'And does he use these things to do magick?'

'So it is said,' I replied, 'but I've never seen any

performed.' And I told her about Beth saying that it was only Mr Kelly who ever saw angels – and also about being mistaken for a wraith the first night I'd stayed at the house.

She laughed, then said, 'They say that magicians seek to discover that elixir called *acqua vitae*.'

'What do those words mean?' I asked, very interested, for that was the expression, the very strange expression, I'd heard spoken by Dr Dee and Mr Kelly.

'I believe they are Latin,' Isabelle said, 'and mean a magick liquid which will make the old young again. They say if you can only discover and drink it, 'twill give you eternal youth.'

'I believe it was that very thing which the queen asked about,' I said wonderingly.

The horse slowed down a little on some stony ground and Isabelle turned right round and looked at me. 'You heard the queen speak of it?'

I nodded. 'I will tell of the circumstances in a moment,' I said. 'She asked Dr Dee if he had yet prepared any.'

'That may well be so, for they say she's ageing fast and mislikes it very much, for she's always adored having men admire her.'

We both considered this for a moment: the notion of the queen being vain, like an ordinary woman, and about her having cares concerning how she appeared to men.

'And there is something more,' I said. 'Dr Dee let

her see a strange crystal ball of his, which is usually kept locked up.'

'I've heard of that!' Isabelle said. 'When I've been working in the Green Man I've heard men discussing it.'

'What do they say?' I asked eagerly.

''Tis called a show-stone and they say miraculous things can be seen in't.'

'Well,' I declared with some importance, 'I have held the very object in my hand!'

She gasped.

'I looked deep into it and saw . . .' I hesitated; what was it that I'd seen? 'A lot of blue and sparkling stones, and something like a flask, or a bottle.'

Startled, Isabelle pulled in the reins of the horse so that it almost stopped, then regarded me fearfully. 'You saw something within it? You have the Sight?'

I shook my head quickly, for the question smacked of witchcraft and such talk was dangerous, even between friends. 'I don't think so,' I said, 'for I never had it before I came to the magician's house.' As I spoke, though, I remembered the strange feeling I'd had on approaching the dark house. Remembered, too, the dreams I'd sometimes had.

'But Dr Dee must have the Sight,' Isabelle said. '*He* must have magickal powers.'

I shrugged. 'I'm certain that he's exceeding clever,' I said, 'but I'm not sure that he has . . .' And I told her the whole story of the queen's visit to the house and how I'd hidden in the fireplace and been discovered by her fool (who had called me pretty, I could not resist adding), about the gentleman who'd wanted to contact his daughter, and how I'd been asked to be a stand-in for her.

She listened intently to my story, asked questions which I did my best to answer, and our journey was almost done by the time I'd finished. 'Would you have done what I would not?' I asked at the end of it.

She thought for a moment, then shook her head. 'I'd do much to possess two gold angels, but would *not* dress up as a dead corpse in a graveyard!' she said and, laughing, pushed her heels into the horse's flanks and we went on.

As we approached Hazelgrove I became much afeared, remembering my nightmare, but as we rode down the main street and I looked across to where our cottage stood, I saw the roof of it and was much relieved. It was still standing there, just as on the day I'd left.

I pointed it out to Isabelle. "Tis very close – but I'd be obliged if you'd go the long way around by the church and across the green, so I can reassure myself that everything else is the same,' I said.

Smiling a little, she said she was happy to go wher-ever I bade her.

As we entered the village I could see that the main street was busy and that a small crowd had gathered by the stocks in front of the church. Feeling a sudden foreboding, I asked Isabelle to pull up the horse some distance away, then slipped down from its back and, after rubbing my aching limbs, walked quietly towards the church, keeping behind the trees as much as I could.

As I approached the stocks I saw that a man was being held there. His head had fallen to one side, his mouth gaped open, and the villagers had taken the opportunity to unload their rotten vegetables on to him, for his face was stained red and there were tomato skins and other foul things in his hair.

He cursed as he sat there, and spat at the ground and groaned – and yet I felt no sympathy for him, for I knew he was probably being justly punished for some wrong-doing. Besides, 'twas not the first time my father had been held so.

I watched him for a moment, and then I silently made my way back to where Isabelle stood beside the horse.

'Someone you know?' she asked, observing my face.

I nodded and told her, and asked if she'd mind if I went to my cottage on my own, for I knew Ma would be deeply ashamed of whatever Father had done, and 'twas not at all the right time to introduce Isabelle to her.

Ma was sitting on a stool outside the cottage, which I found very surprising, for the day was chill for October and a fine drizzle had started to fall. As I approached her I became uneasy, for I saw from the way she sat, slumped, her shoulders drooping, that there was something very wrong.

She looked up, saw me and began to weep, not bursting out with sobs, but crying sad and hopeless tears, as if resuming some misery that had begun long before.

I sat down beside her, not caring that the grass was soaking wet.

'Why are you out here?' I asked. 'Let's go indoors and we can speak properly and you can tell me what's happened.' For I knew already that this must be more than my father being held in the stocks.

She shook her head. 'I can't go in there again,' she said, shaking her head violently. 'No, I cannot. 'Tis all gone. 'Tis hopeless.'

'What d'you mean, all gone?' I asked.

'Quite, quite gone,' was all she said.

I got up, went to the door of our cottage and looked in. And then I knew what she meant, for every last piece of the interior had been removed, right down to the window shutters. Our coffer, the table, every stool and utensil, the ladder which led to the bedroom, even the fire irons and the rusty old cauldron which had always hung over the fire were gone.

The sight was enough to bring tears to my own eyes, for although ours had never been a rich or happy home (and we had Father to thank for this) my brothers and sisters and I had some good times within its walls, and

Ma, despite everything she'd had to contend with, had ever done her best to keep us warm and fed and sheltered. Now the house was just a bleak and empty cell.

I stood there for a moment, then went back to Ma and asked her to tell me what had happened.

'It was because of your father,' she whispered.

'Oh, I know 'tis he who must be behind it all,' I said bitterly. 'Who else *would* it be? But what did he do?'

'Gambled all our money away, every last penny. And afterwards, sold everything in the cottage to pay the debts. He sold my clothes, he sold the window frames, he even sold the wood that I'd been collecting for our winter fires, but he still owed half the men in the Pig and Flute. And he also stole Sam Taylor's sow and sold it at market and took the church poor box.'

'Oh, Ma!' I squeezed her shoulders, held her thin body to mine. 'But what will happen now? What will you do?'

'Your father will be let out of the stocks tomorrow, and then we've been told that we must go to a house of correction.'

'No!' I looked at her in dismay, remembering my dream.

She nodded, sighed. ''Tis all that remains for us.'

'But *you* shouldn't be punished! What have *you* done wrong?'

'The rent on this cottage hasn't been paid since summer, and Lord Ashe's man means to repossess it.'

She began to cry again, rocking backwards and forwards on the stool. 'The shame,' she kept saying. 'Oh, the shame of it!'

I gripped her shoulders. 'Ma,' I said, 'you must try and be strong.' I felt in my pocket but did not have any coin with me, not as much as a penny. 'I'll get some money and send it to you.'

'You couldn't get as much as your father owes!'

'I'll try,' I said, hugging her. 'I'll get every penny I can. And in the meantime you must refuse to leave this cottage. Tell Lord Ashe's man that someone in your family is sending you money this week.'

'But you have not the means . . .' She suddenly seemed to rally a little. 'But Lucy, what are you doing here? Where have you come from?'

'From a little way off,' I said. 'I live in Mortlake and I have a job as nursemaid in a big house.'

She raised a hand to touch my cheek. 'My girl. You've got away from him as you should have done. Ah, I'm proud of you, Lucy. You ever were a canny child.'

I kissed her. 'I'll find the money. I'll not let you down, Ma. I promise.'

She nodded and tried to smile, but I knew she didn't believe me, so I hugged her once more and then fairly ran back to where Isabelle and the horse were waiting.

The journey back was a lot quicker, for the horse seemed to have been warmed up by its earlier jog and took off at a fair gallop all the way. For my part, I was hardly bothered now about my safety and whether I might fall, just concerned that we should return as quickly as possible so that I could do what I had to.

Arriving back, I had a joyous reception from Beth and Merryl, for they seemed to think I might have gone for good, like their other nursemaids. Promising them that I'd tell them the tale of my journey home soon, I took Isabelle to my room and presented her with my apple-green bodice and skirt.

She looked at me, surprised and pleased. 'Why are you giving me these?'

'I was going to give you them anyway,' I said. 'But now I want you to take them in return for another trip to Hazelgrove.'

'You want to go back?' she asked, for I'd told her nothing of Ma's dilemma, just said that she was in a bad way.

'Not I,' I said, 'for I'd not be allowed the time from work. But if you happen to be exercising another horse . . .'

She nodded, wide-eyed. 'I could be.'

'Then there's something I'd like you to take to Hazelgrove for me. Something which I hope to give you tomorrow, which will be of the utmost importance to my ma.'

'Of course,' she said, and folding and tucking the outfit under her arm, she kissed me goodbye, vowing she wouldn't let me down.

I made Beth and Merryl ready for bed, telling a tall

tale of a ride in which I'd got lost in a deep forest, thwarted a highwayman and made friends with a great variety of talking animals. After that I washed my hands and face and made my way to the library, for Mistress Midge had told me that Dr Dee and Mr Kelly had been ensconced there all day. 'And they have twice sent me out for mutton pasties and a jug of ale from the tavern,' she added sourly.

Trembling, for I was afeared they might have changed their minds or found someone else to do the job, I knocked at the black door and waited for permission to enter. When I did so, I saw both men seated at the long table with a number of parchments before them. Behind them, on the wall, were two vast charts. One of them, Merryl had told me, was for plotting the movement of the stars, the other gave the times of the tides all round the world.

'Yes?' Dr Dee asked, looking annoyed at my interruption.

I sank into a curtsey. 'Excuse my boldness in addressing you directly, Sirs,' I said when I straightened up, 'but the other evening you made a proposition. You asked me to take part in a . . . a performance that you intend to put on.'

Mr Kelly started, looking up from his parchments for the first time.

'I refused you then, but now I think I might like to act in this masquerade.'

Dr Dee glanced at Mr Kelly, stroking his beard from

top to bottom. 'You've changed your mind? Why is this?'

'I'll be frank, Sir,' I said, feeling myself blush. 'A member of my family is badly in need of money and I want to help them.'

'I see,' said Dr Dee slowly.

'Not worried about your father's Puritanism now, Lucy?' asked Mr Kelly sardonically.

I shook my head, blushing further. 'I'll do it if you want me to.'

The two men exchanged glances. 'There is still a part for you to play, certainly,' Dr Dee said.

'You mentioned two gold angels, did you not? So if I agree to join the masque, then – begging your pardons – would it be possible for me to have my fee in advance?'

Dr Dee snorted. 'I haven't got so much. How about you, Kelly?'

Mr Kelly somewhat reluctantly produced a small velvet pouch from his pocket. Shaking the contents of this on to the table, he picked up two gold coins and held them out to me, saying, 'In return for these you must promise to do whatever it is we ask of you and vow never to utter a word of it.'

I'd already told Isabelle, of course, but I nodded just the same. 'Yes, Sir, and thank you kindly. When . . . when is it likely that this masque will take place?'

They exchanged glances. 'Next Wednesday would be especially opportune,' said Dr Dee.

Mr Kelly smiled, but I didn't like his smile, for it reminded me of that on the face of the ally-gators. He said, 'Yes, next Wednesday, the thirty-first day of the month.'

I shivered. 'But that date is the Eve of All Hallows, Sir,' I said, for I well knew that on this date all good citizens should keep within their doors, leaving ghouls, witches and other evils free to roam.

'It is. But *you* have nothing to fear, child,' said Mr Kelly.

'Indeed not,' said Dr Dee. 'Unschooled and simple souls can always go abroad on this night, for God in His mercy will protect you from witchcraft.' He waved his hand. 'You may go now.'

Chapter Thirteen

The following morning I went to the hut where Isabelle lived, and gave into her keeping a purse I'd newly sewn. It contained the two pieces of gold and the few copper coins I had left from the money I'd brought with me from home.

"Twill be enough to keep my ma from the poorhouse,' I said to her, and added, 'And my father, too – even though I wouldn't care if *he* never saw the light of day again.'

'I'll take it tomorrow,' she promised. 'And my brother has said he'll ride with me and see that I get there safely. He's grateful, see, for what you've done, for if you'd gone to the Watch when ...'

I hastily told her, not another *word*, and she smiled and put the purse into her pocket. She looked over her shoulder into the hut, where Merryl was playing a staring-out game, as little girls do, with Margaret, the youngest of Isabelle's sisters. 'You've told your gent'men you've decided to take part in the deception, then?' she asked in a low voice and I nodded.

'When will it be?'

'October the thirty-first,' I replied.

Her eyes widened. 'But that's . . .'

I nodded, then tried to make light of it. 'But 'twill be all right; the ghouls and ghosties won't come after me, for they'll think I'm one of them!'

'You shouldn't joke about such things,' she said anxiously. 'Be sure to carry some crossed rowan twigs – and also a moonstone, for that's said to be efficacious against witches. And they say that the sound of a brass bell which has been blessed in church will rid any place of demons in an instant.'

I began laughing. 'If I take all those things I'd be so hung about with charms that I'd be unable to walk!'

The rest of that day I couldn't help but feel greatly afeared – not merely about the date of the masque, but about my purse, for although I liked Isabelle very much and counted her as a friend, that money would mean life or death to my ma. I hadn't ever met Isabelle's brother, so how could I know whether to trust him or not? Would he, on hearing of what the purse contained, be tempted to steal it away?

Mistress Dee visited the kitchen that afternoon, which was only about the second time I'd ever seen her out of her room. She was not attired as a lady should be, but wearing a poor nightgown, her hair hung from under her nightcap in thin wisps. She looked very unhappy, poor lady, for on Dr Dee's insistence, Mistress Allen had taken little Arthur off to his wet nurse early that morning, and there he had stayed.

It was a strange little scene: Beth and Merryl standing one each side of their mother, each holding a hand and talking to her, the cook fussing, trying to coax her mistress to take something nourishing and above this a continual shrieking and a rattling of the cellar door from Tom-fool, who'd been locked down there on account of his making Mistress Dee extremely nervous.

'Would you take a little light chicken gruel, Madam?' said Mistress Midge. 'I could send Lucy out for a boiling fowl.' This only bringing forth a shake of the head from the mistress, she went on, 'Or a little conserve of sage and scabious to aid your melancholy?'

'Thank you,' sighed Mistress Dee, 'but I could not swallow a morsel of food.'

Mistress Midge looked at me in despair, shrugging.

'After child-bed my ma always got my sisters to take a tonic of elderflowers and barberries in claret,' I said tentatively, but Mistress Dee again refused, saying she'd rather not, and even Merryl's offer to make her a plate of gilt gingerbread could not persuade her to change her mind.

'Arthur. Poor wee babe,' she kept saying. 'He won't know where he is or who his mother might be. He'll think I've abandoned him.'

'Begging your pardon, Madam,' Mistress Midge said, 'but the child is far too young to worry about his whereabouts. And a finer wet nurse with such milk in abundance you'll not find anywhere in the county!'

Mistress Dee's eyes closed in anguish. 'Oh, but he's so tiny and helpless,' she sighed. 'And he's our heir!'

'Mama,' asked Merryl suddenly, 'were you this unhappy about leaving me with a wet nurse?

'And *me?*' put in Beth jealously.

Mistress Dee rallied slightly. 'Of course, my darlings,' she said, 'every bit as anxious,' and Mistress Midge caught my eye and gave me a half-wink.

The next day, towards evening, there was a tapping on the kitchen window and I looked out to see little Margaret standing there, proffering a scrap of paper. I took this from her eagerly. I knew that Isabelle could read and also write a little, for she'd been taught her letters by a teacher she'd washed for, and when I studied the paper I found, much to my delight, that I could read the few words she'd written. The note said: *Your ma says you ever were a canny child*, and I knew from this that Isabelle had truly delivered the purse, and that I'd done right to trust her and her brother, even though my heart had misgiven me several times during the day.

After the children's bedtime I was summoned to speak with Dr Dee. Whether Mistress Midge was curious about this interview with my employer or any of the subsequent ones I don't know, but she never questioned me about them or enquired as to what we might be talking about.

In the library, Dr Dee and Mr Kelly were sitting one each side of the large fireplace, looking at me seriously.

'Lucy, we must rehearse your part,' Dr Dee said, when I'd wished them a good evening.

'Indeed, Sir,' I said, and tried to sound keen and biddable, so that they wouldn't suspect that I knew the real reason for the masquerade. 'What must I do?'

'We want you to impersonate the daughter of Lord Vaizey, who's an important personage at the Court of Her Majesty.'

I nodded slowly.

'We have obtained various descriptions of this young lady, who was about your age . . .'

'She *was*, Sir?'

'She has passed over to the land of shadows,' said Mr Kelly soberly.

'I am to pretend to be a dead girl?' I asked in a shocked voice. 'That seems a very strange masquerade . . .'

'Whether it is or not is no business of yours,' said Mr Kelly curtly.

'You must understand that the grieving father will be much comforted by seeing his daughter again,' said Dr Dee.

'I see. So I am to pretend to be her.' I allowed a moment's silence, as if taking all this in, and then asked what words I'd need to play my part.

'You'll need to learn very little,' said Dr Dee. 'You'll

appear, Lord Vaizey will speak and ask for your forgiveness, and then you'll say, *"I forgive you, Father."*'

'Just that?'

They both nodded. 'Try it, child,' Dr Dee said.

'*I forgive you, Father,*' I intoned.

'With more feeling!' urged Mr Kelly.

'And softer, more cultured.'

I tried again. '*I forgive you, Father.*'

Dr Dee shook his head. 'You have an ugly country twang to your voice.'

'Remember, the young woman – Alice – was maid of honour to the queen,' said Mr Kelly. 'Your voice should be well-modulated, sweet and low.'

'*I forgive you, Father,*' I said breathily.

'Again and yet again,' Mr Kelly said curtly, 'until we're satisfied.'

'You must work hard at it, for two gold coins are not as easily earned as all that,' put in Dr Dee.

Thirty gold coins certainly seemed to be, I thought, but of course could not say this. Instead I asked, 'But what if the man, her father, seeks to question me more?'

Mr Kelly said very sternly that I was to say nothing more than the words they were tutoring me in. 'You will appear, say what you've been taught and then vanish. Do you understand?'

'Try again,' Dr Dee said, 'for there is much depends on this.'

'*I forgive you, Father.*'

'That's a little better.'

'Again – and then once again.'

And so the evening passed.

Going into the library the following night, I was told I'd have to wear a winding sheet for the masquerade, so that it would appear I'd just stepped out of my coffin.

'This won't be of rough wool as the common people have,' Mr Kelly assured me, 'but a cloth of fine white linen. And you may keep it after.'

I shuddered, picturing the scene and wondering if any real ghosts and ghouls abroad that night would be angry at this deception, and was only slightly appeased by the thought of the good white linen sheet which would be mine to keep.

I asked them how I'd be able to walk properly; how I'd appear and disappear with a sheet wound tightly around my person, and the two gentlemen, after some discussion, decided that the sheet could be loose around me, creating a flowing effect. Underneath I'd wear a nightdress of high quality.

'But we must find out what *sort* of a nightdress,' Dr Dee said worriedly to Mr Kelly. 'If the girl was put into the grave wearing spotted muslin, then she mustn't appear wearing tucked lawn.'

'Indeed,' said Mr Kelly.

'And how would she have had her hair?' Dr Dee suddenly asked. 'What *colour* was it?'

They looked at each other, and then at me.

'We must find out and, if necessary, obtain a wig,'

said Dr Dee.

'Or perhaps tie her hair back, put it up out of sight. She was a married woman, after all. She would have worn it up.'

It was then, just at that moment, that I heard a voice close to me say, quite clearly, 'Alas, poor Alice. I was a married woman, yet died a maid.'

I looked round in surprise, for it seemed to me that someone must have come into the room. And then, there being no one there, and the two gentlemen not appearing to have noticed anything amiss, I realised that the voice had been in my head. And with it was the image of a girl wearing a white gown, with long fair hair about her shoulders and a wreath of myrtle on her head.

This all struck me as very strange. And strangest of all was that the image of the girl was not before me, like a looking-glass reflection, but that when I looked down at myself, *I* seemed to be the one wearing the white gown and wreath. What was more, the silk of the night-dress was clinging to my skin, soaking wet, and a strand of waterweed was trailing from my shoulder.

'She was a maid,' I heard myself saying.

Both gentlemen looked at me in astonishment.

'And wore her hair hanging loose . . .'

'What . . . what do you mean?' asked Dr Dee.

'How can you possibly know anything about her?' said the other. 'Besides, she was not a maid, for she was married.'

'But . . . I think . . . the marriage was not a complete one,' I said in a rush, for the image and the voice had vanished, leaving me wondering how I could possibly have known any of these things, especially the latter, most intimate notion.

'The marriage was unconsummated?' Dr Dee asked.

I blushed red. 'If you'll pardon me, Sir, 'twas my fancy that it was.'

'Tush!' said Mr Kelly. 'A girl like you can know nothing at all about such things.'

Two days later I was summoned to the library during the day and found both gentlemen sitting there waiting. They told me to hide myself behind a tapestry and to listen to what was being said by a third party who was arriving shortly, for it would be advantageous to me.

Intrigued, I did as I was bid and a short while after a woman was ushered into the room. I peered around one side of the tapestry but could not see her face, for she was wearing a long cloak with its hood up. She seemed a middling sort of person, however, for the material of her cloak was of some quality and she had good leather shoes.

'You are Mistress . . . well, we shall call you Mistress X,' said Dr Dee.

The woman didn't reply and I wondered if she was looking all around her in wonder, as I had when I'd first come to the library.

'You were a maidservant at the house of Lord Vaizey?'

'I was, Sir,' said the woman nervously.

'You needn't fear us. We shall tell no one of your visit here,' Dr Dee said. 'Besides, 'tis all for Lord Vaizey's benefit, for we are seeking to help cure his melancholy at his daughter's demise.'

'I believe you attended on Mistress Alice sometimes?' Mr Kelly asked.

'I did, Sir,' said the woman. 'When her personal maid was indisposed I would attend her at home, or at Richmond Palace, and I would dress her hair or lay out her clothes.' Her voice began to shake, 'And a lovelier young lady you never saw in all your life.'

'Quite,' said Mr Kelly. 'And we want to know a little more about her . . .'

'So that we may be of help to her poor father in his hour of need,' Dr Dee put in. He coughed, 'Her appearance, for instance. You said you used to dress her hair?'

'Lovely hair, she had! Thick and golden. Like corn in the sunshine, I used to say.'

'And she wore it . . . plaited up?'

'She wore it down, Sir! It curled right down below her shoulders.'

'Interesting, interesting,' said Dr Dee. 'And how did she walk? Small steps or long strides?'

'Little steps – she was light and graceful on her feet and almost seemed to glide along.'

'And her voice?' asked Mr Kelly.

'Very light and clear. She spoke six languages!' came the reply. 'And she could paint, play the lute, dance, embroider and sew quilts. Oh, she had every womanly virtue!'

'She sounds a delightful young lady,' said Dr Dee. 'Such a sad loss for Lord Vaizey.'

'Such a loss for us all,' said the woman. 'Why, Lord Vaizey should never have insisted on that marriage!' As she said this she seemed to check herself. 'Begging your pardon, Sirs, but she was a bonny girl and we all loved her.'

'For certain,' said Dr Dee.

'She loved us, too – and she was completely devoted to the queen. Why, she would have walked through fire for Her Grace.'

Mr Kelly pulled a coin from his pocket and began flicking it into the air and catching it again. 'And there's nothing more about her appearance we should know? Her complexion, for instance. Perhaps she had freckles, or marks from the smallpox?'

'Oh, no, Sir! Her skin was as smooth as silk. Pale, too. Like a lady's should be.'

'And her eyes – dark?'

'Blue, sir. Blue as speedwell.'

'Ah,' said Mr Kelly, and he was probably thinking of my eyes, which were not.

'And is there anything else at all? For instance, did she like nice fabrics?'

'Sir?'

'Silks and satins?' Mr Kelly flicked the coin further into the air, where it was deftly caught by the woman. 'Or did she prefer the more homely feel of cotton and linen?'

'Well, as I said, she was a real lady,' the woman said, pocketing the coin. 'She would wear nothing but pure silk next to her skin. Why, her mother had a dozen silken nightgowns made for her marriage chest!'

'White, I daresay . . .'

'Cream, sir. A rich clotted cream to suit her pale complexion. She was buried in one such a gown, Sir.'

'Aah,' said Dr Dee and Mr Kelly together.

'And she died on her wedding day?' Dr Dee asked after a moment.

I saw the woman dab her nose with a kerchief. 'She did,' she sniffed. 'That very afternoon, after the ceremony, while folks were still making merry.'

'So she . . . died still a maid?'

'That's right, Sir. She was buried with her lovely hair loose down her back, and eighteen maids from the poorhouse accompanied the corpse – one for every year of her age – all in black gowns and carrying leather gloves,' said the woman, whose tongue had been somewhat loosened since pocketing the coin. ''Twas all done very fine: the hearse cloth was of purple velvet bordered with blue, which Her Grace herself sent, and there was a big funeral feast after with venison, capons and rabbits.'

My heart was beating very fast. How had I known

that she'd died a maid?

'Sad. Extremely sad,' said Mr Kelly. 'And how did the poor girl die?'

'She drowned, sir,' came the reply. 'There's a fast brook runs through the grounds of her father's house, and she laid herself down in this and floated away. Her body was found trapped in the rushes some time later that evening and though they tried to restore her to life, she was quite, quite dead.'

She began to sob then, which fortunately hid the little cry of surprise I'd given. So *that* was why I'd seen her so in my vision: Alice, poor Alice, with her clothes clinging to her, wet and draped in waterweed . . .

Chapter Fourteen

O n the thirty-first of October a carriage arrived in the dead of night to take me, Dr Dee and Mr Kelly to what I later found out was the churchyard beside the royal chapel at the palace of Richmond, where Alice Vaizey was buried. Dressed in nothing but a cream silk nightdress and cloak, and wearing a long, fair wig, I was hustled into the carriage without ceremony, Mr Kelly heaving me up like a bundle of old clothes and lifting me in, then insisting that I lay flat on the floor so that I could neither see nor be seen.

These precautions seemed unnecessary to me, for the bellman had already called that it was past eleven o'clock and, the night being the dread date that it was, I was sure no one would be abroad. Only the undead; only wraiths and spectres, I thought, and felt for the rowan twigs I'd concealed in the pocket of my cloak.

Isabelle had given me these and told me that if I saw anything supernatural I should hold them out and make the sign of the cross. I'd reminded her, of course, that we weren't supposed to make that sign now, for 'twas a Papist practice, and she'd replied, laughing nervously, saying that the ghosts wouldn't tell on me.

It was the first time I'd ridden in a carriage and it was not at all how I'd imagined such a journey, for it proved to be both beastly and uncomfortable. Being unable to see where I was going made me feel sick in the head and I was so close to the road that I felt every jolt and shake as the carriage lurched from one side to the other, bruising and grazing me as it did so. The hooves of the horses were muffled so that they made hardly a sound going over the cobbled streets, and the driver – whom I didn't see – spoke not a word. I thought that it might be Old Jake, who was a family retainer and who sometimes did odd jobs for Dr Dee, but I never found out.

When the carriage eventually stopped I had to wait while a wooden box was taken off, then told to go hide myself somewhere on the far side of the churchyard. I could see my way, for the moon was almost full, and shivered as I stepped between white tombstones and low-branched yew trees which seemed to have formed themselves into strange and forbidding shapes: one a gargoyle, one a frog, the next a crouching beast.

Going out of the gate on the far side of the church-yard, I marvelled at how everything I looked at seemed, through my overwrought imagination, to have taken on another, more ghastly aspect: the red petals on a drooping flower looked like drops of blood; some twisted, fallen branches on the ground seemed more like bones; and the sound of the light wind coming through the leaves on the trees could have been a coven of witches whispering spells. The moon glimmered, appearing and disappearing between heavy clouds, and I pressed myself against the churchyard wall, saying a prayer to myself, a childish thing I used to chant with my sisters on nights like these:

Each ghoul and ghostie, faery, sprite,
Stay away from me this night
No beaste or goblin, wicked gnome
Is ever welcome in our home.

As I chanted, I wished for a more powerful amulet than the crossed rowan twigs I had in my cloak, wished that I'd managed to procure all the other charms that Isabelle had recommended, for what good would childish rhymes be against true evil?

Dr Dee and Mr Kelly went to and fro, unpacking things from the wooden chest and appearing, by the flickering light of candle-lanterns and in their billowing cloaks, as strange, shadowy creatures. Under these cloaks they wore dark gowns, and, on their heads, velvet skullcaps bearing symbols – the correct attire, I supposed, for the necromancers they purported to be.

I heard some of what they said to each other, for they mentioned giving Lord Vaizey 'what he expected' and 'putting on a show', and I thought to myself that they must consider me very simple indeed if they imagined that I didn't know what they were doing.

Dr Dee drew a large chalk circle on the paved ground with the aid of a strange steel object which bent in the middle. This circle was ruled off by him into very precise lines, and I later saw that these lines formed a five-pointed star, identical to the one I'd seen chalked on the tomb in Mortlake. (Beth told me some days later that this mathematical shape was called a pentacle and was used by magicians as protection, for it was believed that the dark forces couldn't harm anyone who was standing inside such a one.)

When this circle shape was finished, Mr Kelly came across to where I was waiting. He asked me to take off my cloak, then wrapped the winding sheet around me loosely and arranged my false hair over it.

'Your grave-clothes must trail behind you at the back as if you've just risen from the coffin,' he said. 'But be careful not to let the sheet trip you up, and do remember that Mistress Vaizey walked gracefully and had good carriage.'

I nodded. 'When must I appear, Sir?'

'After the ceremony,' he replied.

I looked at him, puzzled.

'There will be a . . . a preliminary when Dr Dee and I will act out a small play,' he explained. 'Following this, you'll hear Dr Dee say the words, "*Arise, sweet spirit!*"'

'And it's then that I am to come into view?'

He nodded. 'You enter by this gate, walk towards us – around this large yew tree – and stand in the chalked symbol in an attitude of prayer, as we've discussed previously. And then Lord Vaizey will speak and ask you to forgive him, and you will say . . . ?'

'*I forgive you, Father.*'

He nodded. 'Then you may look at him beseechingly for just a moment – but do not venture any closer for fear he should notice the colour of your eyes! – and turn and go back behind the yew tree, where Alice's grave lies.'

I nodded. '*Alas, poor Alice,*' said the voice in my head.

I didn't know what time it was, but they say that midnight is the hour when graves give up their dead, so I suppose that it must have been about that time when I heard the muffled thud of a horse's hooves at the front of the church and the light jingle of a bridle.

I began to shake with fright. '*Each ghoul or ghostie, faery, sprite . . .*' I said to myself, but it wasn't just these I was worried about. Suppose Lord Vaizey didn't believe I was his daughter's ghost? Suppose he reached for me and discovered I was real, substantial, not a spirit at all? It wouldn't help me to say that I was working under Dr Dee's instructions; I could still be burnt at the stake as a witch.

A horse and rider came into view and I shrank back against the churchyard wall and watched as the man slipped off his horse. The moon reappeared, allowing me to see that Lord Vaizey – for it must be he – wore a heavy cloak, high boots and a black felt hat with a sable mourning feather. He walked towards Dr Dee and Mr Kelly, and they all exchanged low bows.

Lord Vaizey seemed very anxious, for he was continually wringing his hands and shifting his weight from leg to leg. 'I beg you, gentlemen, tell me straightaway,' he asked hoarsely, 'do we ask too much of my daughter?'

'How so, Sir?' Dr Dee replied.

'Will she mind being called from her eternal sleep? We beg our dead to rest in peace . . . should we leave her to do just that?'

I froze, listening intently.

Mr Kelly spoke up very quickly, no doubt thinking of the thirty gold angels to be gained or lost. 'Not at all, my Lord,' he said. 'Your daughter knows your suffering.'

'And if she can ease that suffering, then I believe she would be willing to do so,' Dr Dee added.

'But suppose she has *not* forgiven me?'

There was a moment's silence, then Dr Dee spoke again. 'I am convinced that she will have, Sir.'

'Do you say so?'

'I am completely sure of it.'

'And I believe she's e'en now waiting to be called by

us,' said Mr Kelly, making a sweeping gesture towards the chalk circle.

Lord Vaizey breathed out with a long sigh and I believe a purse was handed over at this stage, for I saw Mr Kelly slip something into his pocket. The three of them walked towards the chalk circle, then Dr Dee placed himself in its centre, with Mr Kelly and Lord Vaizey standing a little way off, on the other side of the circle from where I was standing.

Dr Dee began bowing to each corner of the grave-yard: low, reverential bows, his arms raised to heaven between each one.

'Dr Dee is preparing to entice your daughter's spirit to return to earth from the heavenly chambers in which she now dwells,' explained Mr Kelly.

'I pray he succeeds,' said Lord Vaizey. 'For I can live no longer with my guilt.'

'You must understand, my Lord, that if he manages to raise her, she'll be an ethereal being; an insubstantial wraith. You mustn't touch her, or even come too close.'

Lord Vaizey didn't reply to this. He seemed too distressed.

'If you disobey these rules, if you *do* touch her,' went on Mr Kelly, 'I must warn you that her soul may be in danger.'

'I won't touch her,' came the hoarse promise.

There was a moment's complete silence.

'Then call in the elements!' Dr Dee declared, and Mr Kelly produced five small pewter bowls from somewhere outside my vision. The first contained something which he set alight, saying as he did so, 'Fire!' The next held water, then came air, spirit and earth. Each bowl was placed at one point of the star.

'The circle of a pentacle protects and contains,' Dr Dee intoned. 'It symbolises eternity and infinity, the cycle of life. The circle touching all five elements indicates their connection.'

'So be it,' responded Mr Kelly.

'Tonight is an auspicious time for a ceremony such as this, for departed spirits will not be far from earth and are ever watching o'er their loved ones . . .'

As this discourse continued I used the time to prepare myself for my entrance, breathing evenly and trying to remember everything about Mistress Vaizey that I'd learned. In a moment I'd take a few steps into the churchyard, give Lord Vaizey a sympathetic glance, utter four short words, and it would be over.

As Dr Dee neared the end of his speech, a cloud of sulphur-tinged smoke began billowing from near the church porch. I was frightened by this at first, thinking it to be something other-worldly, then realised that it was only some stage-setting, a 'mystical' backdrop set up by Dr Dee and Mr Kelly. This was confirmed to me when Mr Kelly pointed at it in wonder, saying, 'The spirits hear us! Oh, see the spirits rising!'

Dr Dee raised his hands to heaven once more and I saw that in his right hand he had the black and silver mirror. 'If you are close to our earth, Alice Vaizey, then hear your father's plea and return through this glass!' he called into the air.

I began to shake with fright.

Dr Dee turned in my direction.

'Alice Vaizey! Arise, sweet spirit!' he commanded, and as he spoke to give me my cue to appear, something very strange happened: a warmth ran through my limbs and I became filled with both calm and courage. Completely in control of myself now, I pulled myself up to my full height, tossed my hair back from my shoulders and walked lightly through the smoke until I reached the pentacle. I was on one side of it, Lord Vaizey on the other.

I stood as I'd been tutored, head slightly lowered now so that he couldn't see my face too clearly, hands folded as if in prayer, and waited for the smoke to clear.

When it shifted slightly, there was a gasp from Lord Vaizey, a throaty cry of, 'Alice!'

I nodded meekly.

'Alice! Oh, let me . . .' Lord Vaizey took a step towards me, arms outstretched, and had to be restrained by Mr Kelly.

'Lord Vaizey, please,' he said, 'remember what we have told you. Remember that it could be dangerous for your daughter's soul . . .'

'Ah yes,' said Lord Vaizey. I stole a glance at him and saw – poor man – that there were tears coursing down his face.

'Say what you wish to say swiftly, my Lord, for her

time on earth will be but brief,' said Dr Dee.

'Alice, Alice!' said Lord Vaizey brokenly. 'I only gave you in marriage because I thought it for the best.'

I let my head fall to one side, as if considering this.

'I . . . I imagined that you would come to love him in time, but if I had known you were that unhappy, I would never have forced the marriage upon you.'

I waited another moment, head still bowed.

'I was a selfish and unfeeling man!' he said. 'Oh, child, just tell me that you forgive me.'

I paused again for a count of five, then looked up and said my words: '*I forgive you, Father.*'

'Oh, bless you, child!' cried Lord Vaizey, and I heard Dr Dee breathe out, a long rasping breath.

Mr Kelly said with some relief, 'Hallelujah! You are forgiven indeed, Sir!' and I was about to turn and go back when I felt the heat course through me again and I heard myself saying with some urgency, ''Tis too late for me, but save my lady!'

From Dr Dee and Mr Kelly there came a shocked silence.

Lord Vaizey looked at me, baffled and at a loss. 'My dear,' he began. 'What do you speak of? What do you mean?'

In my head I saw myself holding the crystal ball – the seeing stone – again, and spying the jewelled flask within it. 'You must save my royal lady!' I cried.

Dr Dee raised the mirror in the air. 'Sweet spirit! Haste ye back from whence you came!' he cried, and his words acted like cold water on the warmth and energy that had coursed through me so that I became myself again.

Turning, I walked back through the smoke. Why I had spoken thus, I had no idea.

Chapter Fifteen

'Y ou fool-born idiot – you could have ruined things for all of us!' said Dr Dee angrily.

'Not only that; you could have condemned us to death!' Mr Kelly raged. 'We could have all ended up hung, drawn and quartered.'

I flinched under their looks but managed to answer steadily. 'How so?' I said. 'For wasn't last night just an entertainment?'

Mr Kelly waved me off angrily. 'Less of your impudence!' he barked. 'Dr Dee should dismiss you for disobedience and lack of respect.'

It was the morning after the raising of Mistress Vaizey and I'd been asked to attend upon the two gentlemen in the library. On the journey back the previous night we hadn't spoken of the matter, for they'd been too intent on getting home swiftly and undetected. Besides, Mr Kelly had said that he couldn't trust himself to speak to me, so angry was he.

'You knew what your words were to be; who gave you the authority to say more?' he asked now, while Dr Dee stood by, simply shaking his head and running his hands along his beard. 'Whatever possessed you to say such things?'

'I just felt that the young lady I was speaking for wanted me to . . .' I said helplessly.

'What nonsense!' He turned to Dr Dee. 'This is what you get, Dee, if you ask someone simple and unschooled to undertake an important task.'

'We had very little choice,' said Dr Dee tersely.

'Girls such as she are of a shallow, flighty nature and allow their imaginations to run away with them,' Mr Kelly continued, pacing about the room. 'Their girlish fancies cause them to forget the directions of their elders. A girl of this standard and this class cannot possibly be trusted.'

'You may be right,' Dr Dee shrugged, 'but I still say we had no choice.'

'And what is her excuse and explanation? *She felt the young lady wanted her to . . .*' he finished, cruelly mimicking my country accent.

I hung my head, knowing better than to speak up for myself and risk losing my position in the household. I could explain no further, however, bar to say that something – someone – had compelled me to speak as I had done. And it was obvious to me who that someone was.

* * *

I yawned frequently as I managed my chores that day, and although cook gave me many sidelong glances and more than once called me a slugabed and a lazy strumpet, she didn't ask why I was so tired. The mistress was abed again, weary and ailing, so that in the afternoon Mistress Midge sent me and the children to the market to buy some elderflowers and tansy, for she had a mind to make her a tonic. I went off eagerly, for I thought the walk might clear my head a little, and I also very much wanted to see Isabelle.

My friend was sitting on a wooden box in the marketplace, selling produce. 'White cabbage, white young cabbage!' she called. 'White cabbage, fine and white!'

'Isabelle is back wearing your bodice and skirt again,' Beth said in a loud whisper as we approached.

I shushed her. 'They are her own now. I've given them to her and you must say no more about them.'

She looked at me, wide-eyed, but said nothing. Margaret was there also, sitting on the box beside Isabelle and selling walnuts, so we sent all the children off to play together so that we could talk.

'I'm so very glad to see you, for I couldn't sleep last night for thinking of you in the churchyard!' she said. I sat down beside her and she gave me a hug. 'Do tell what happened, for I swear I can't wait another moment.' Without pausing for breath she went on, 'But if it's a tale of devils and black dogs then I pray you leave out the worst, or I shall ne'er sleep again!'

I smiled a little at that. 'No dogs. I survived and am here.'

'And what terrors did you see?'

'I saw none – but I was extremely afeared and wouldn't do it again – no, not even for *four* gold coins.'

'And did the man they were duping believe in you? Did he truly think he was speaking to the wraith of his daughter?'

I nodded. 'I believe so . . .'

I paused in my tale as a housewife stopped in front of us, picked up one of the cabbages and squeezed it, then put it down again, shaking her head.

'But something more occurred,' I said as soon as the woman was out of earshot. 'Something strange happened so that I found myself saying more than I should have done.'

She looked at me, puzzled. 'Why should you have done such a thing?'

'That's just it – I don't know,' I answered. 'I was arrayed in my grave-clothes and appeared just as I was supposed to. The girl's father spoke to ask forgiveness, I said my part, then . . . then instead of vanishing, I told them that it was too late for me, but that they must save the life of the queen.'

Isabelle pulled herself away from me, looking at me strangely. '*Save the queen?*'

I nodded. 'And . . . and at the same time I saw the image I'd seen in the show-stone: the jewelled flask. It has something to do with that, but I don't know what.'

Isabelle shook her head. 'I mislike this.'

'So do I.' My hands twisted together nervously. 'But I feel that this message is with me now; is mine to pass on. It . . . it's as if it's been given into my safekeeping.'

'What did you actually say? The exact words?'

I had no trouble remembering: *''Tis too late for me, but save my lady. Save my royal lady!'*

'And you are quite sure that you were talking of the queen?'

I nodded emphatically. 'Alice Vaizey was maid of honour to the queen. She would have laid down her life for Her Grace.' As most of us would, if asked, I thought to myself.

'And doesn't your master – doesn't Dr Dee – seem inclined to do anything about this message?'

I shook my head. 'They think it's merely a girlish fancy on my part. A wish to make myself sound more important.'

'Well.' Isabelle thought for a moment. 'Can't you just forget about it?'

'I've been trying to,' I said wryly, 'but I don't think it's going to let me.'

I had another vivid dream that night. Not about Ma this time, but one in which I saw our queen lying on a bed hung with black velvet curtains, while above her was placed a wooden shield which bore the royal coat of arms draped in black sarcenet. Twelve maidens knelt around the bed, the sounds of sobbing filled the air and there was solemn music playing, so that I knew she must be dead. As I looked on, one of the kneeling girls turned and stared straight at me, and I knew in my soul it was Alice Vaizey.

'Lucy,' said the image, 'I cannot, but *you* must save my lady.'

'And how shall I do that?' I asked her. 'For no one will listen to a low-born maid.'

'You must try. You must save my royal lady!' she said again, more urgently, and I remember feeling the great weight of this responsibility, and, weeping and struggling, trying to get away from the room in which the body of the queen lay, and in doing this I succeeded in waking myself up.

I thought long about the matter and, Dr Dee being on his own that morning, I went to him to recount the dream. I'd thought that perhaps he'd take note of it and tell me what it meant, for the well-to-do citizens of the town consulted him on their dreams regularly, seeking to know if a certain one was a good portent or no. My employer was hard into a book, however, for a new and seemingly important volume had arrived that day, and hardly noticed my presence in the room until I made it felt.

'Excuse my presumption, Sir,' I began, standing full square before his desk, 'but I've had a dream which I feel may be of some import.'

He didn't raise his head but merely waved a hand to dismiss me.

''Twas about the queen, Sir, and her safety.'

He glanced up for an instant. 'Not that again.'

'But it seems most important to me, Sir, and in my childhood I often had dreams which . . .'

His attention returned once more to the book and he began tracing along a line of strange symbols with his fingers. 'I've already heard these attempts to draw attention to yourself. I'll have you know that there's no more money forthcoming.'

'I don't speak for the sake of money, Sir, but for love of our queen!' I said with some indignation.

'Begone!' he said. 'Or I shall do what Mr Kelly suggests and dismiss you from the house.'

I opened my mouth to speak further but then gave up and turned away. I'd realised that it was just as I'd thought all along: that it was only the dreams of the wealthy and powerful that were significant; the dreams of servant girls were as nothing.

Another day went by before I could get out to try to see Isabelle, and by that time I'd had the dream again, exactly as before. But I couldn't find her at the market that morning and was told by a woman selling pies that she was at home, boiling up candle ends, and would be there on the morrow.

Another night meant another dream, every detail the same as before, and it came to me that I was going to continue having this dream until I acted upon it. Until I acted on it – or until something terrible happened to the queen . . .

Going to market the following morning I found Isabelle at her usual spot near the well and selling not cabbages nor lavender wands, but wax candles made from scraps and stub-ends of the old. 'White wax candles for one ha'penny!' she was calling. 'Light your way with fine white candles!'

I smiled as I approached her. 'If a maid waited long enough, she would find you selling everything she ever wanted to buy.'

She laughed, patted the box beside her and I sat down. 'Is all well with you?' she asked with some concern. 'You look very pale.'

'I do feel somewhat strange,' I admitted. And I told her about the dreams concerning the queen, and how I felt I should do something, *longed* to do something, but couldn't think what this should be. 'I've tried to speak to Dr Dee,' I said, 'but now that he no longer needs me for his masque, he hardly bothers to acknowledge my presence in a room, much less listens to me.'

'What are you going to do, then?'

I shrugged. 'What indeed?'

'Maybe you should take heed of the dreams and go and warn the queen.'

I looked at her and could not help but laugh. 'Oh, of course! I'll go to the palace to seek an audience. The queen will receive me graciously and offer refreshment, and then I'll tell her the whole story.'

'That may be the only way,' Isabelle said seriously. She closed her eyes for a moment as if she was thinking hard. 'Are you sure you aren't cursed with the Sight?'

I shook my head and then looked at her sideways, somewhat embarrassed to confess. 'But – well, I have sometimes dreamed of things which later came true,' I admitted.

'You have?'

'As a child, yes.'

'So what if coming to live in the magician's house has somehow enhanced that gift.'

I stared at her. 'There is another thing: I share the same birthday as Alice Vaizey,' I said.

'Which surely means there is a further link between you – that is, if those astrologers who cast birth charts are right.'

I was silent, thinking.

'We have a wise fool living in our hamlet,' Isabelle confided, 'an old woman who sometimes speaks perfect sense and at other times babbles without meaning. Once she told me that the spirits of the dead are unable to leave the earth if they still have work to do on it.'

I looked at her with some considerable interest.

'What if Alice Vaizey, feeling that the queen is in danger, is unable to move on to a higher state?' she asked.

'Might such a thing be possible?'

'I've heard it said that the veil between this world and the next is but wafer thin, and that sometimes – in times of need – it can disappear altogether. Perhaps, by pretending to be Alice Vaizey, you've somehow attracted her spirit to yours. Perhaps she's trying to speak through you.'

'Through me . . .'

'Isn't that just what Mr Kelly does – gives the dead voices? They talk through him, do they not?'

'He says so.' I thought about this fantastical supposition for a moment. 'Even so, what can I do?' I asked helplessly. And then added, 'Unless I could write and tell the queen that I believe her life to be in danger . . .'

Isabelle shrugged. 'Her life is permanently in danger from those who would put her cousin on the throne. Besides, you and I are not capable of penning a letter which would merit the queen's attention. 'Twould just be dismissed as the ravings of a mad person.'

I sighed. 'And neither do I own parchment nor pen.'

'So you will have to go and seek an audience with her!'

'And how should I do that?'

'There's a way,' she said, 'for every Sunday when Her Grace is in residence in Richmond she passes through the Presence Chamber, and it's there that the public gather to petition her or just to look upon her and see some of the wonders of her reign: the fine tapestries, paintings and furniture she's collected.'

'I've heard of that,' I said. 'But can anyone go? Could I go?'

She nodded. 'Of course. And you'd not be alone, for I'd go with you. I've long wanted to see inside the palace!'

'So I'd try to speak to her . . .' The whole idea was exceeding alarming. But then, if I ever again wanted to have a sound night's sleep without dreams of death, it seemed that I might have to attend on the queen at Richmond Palace.

Chapter Sixteen

During the next week, Alice Vaizey stole into my head at every opportunity. I dreamed of her at night and she crept up on me during the day, whether I was playing with the children, scouring the pots with sand or listening to Mistress Midge berate some poor tradesman or other. I could hear her voice whispering in the trees, '*Alas, poor Alice*', or pleading, '*Save my lady!*' within the clip-clop rhythm of the hooves of passing horses. She had entered my life and did not seem inclined to move from it.

The days were growing shorter, the weather danker, and despite the various tonics which cook had prepared, Mistress Dee seemed not to be improving. To stir her from her lethargy, therefore, Mistress Midge proposed that she should take an excursion to see her mother, the dowager, who still lived in the family house in Greenwich. Even this might not have stirred her, but for the fact that Mistress Midge also suggested that the babe be brought from his wet nurse so that he, along with his sisters, could visit his maternal grandmother. Dr Dee was to go as well, which rather surprised me, but I heard from the children that Mr Kelly had gone to Nottinghamshire to scry for lost treasure, so presumed that my employer must have time on his hands.

A boat and waterman were hired, for the journey to Greenwich was to be made by river, and it was arranged that they would travel on the Saturday and come back late on the Monday. The boat was just large enough for five, so the only servant going would be Mistress Allen. This was very good news for me, for it meant that I'd be able to go on my own excursion.

I asked Mistress Midge for the Sunday off, telling her that I was going to try and set eyes on the queen and see her fine possessions, and she didn't demur at this, no doubt thinking of the cronies she'd have over to gossip and share a few mugs of ale with while the house was empty.

In the market place on Friday, Isabelle and I made final plans. What we should wear was the most consuming question, for people went in their costliest gowns and jewellery and competed with each other as to who could look the wealthiest and most fashionable. She said, too, that the palace guards were fussy about who was allowed through the gates and kept out beggars, the poorer sort and anyone who smelled.

I giggled, sniffing the air. 'Then today they wouldn't

allow you in!' I said, for that day she was selling herrings from a basket. These herrings, unfortunately, had come downriver from the city in a barge and taken a day or so in the travelling, so were not at their freshest.

She looked at me impishly. 'But this is a goodly catch, for I've bought the herrings ten for a penny and am selling them at a penny each!' She continued, 'And I shall scrub my hands with soapwort tonight, rub them afterwards with rose water, and tomorrow be dressed as fine as everyone else.'

I laughed, for a moment forgetting the seriousness of my mission. 'And so shall I!'

'We'll see some excellent sights, Lucy,' she continued, 'for people going to the palace will do anything in order to be noticed by Her Grace. They say the very sight of the clothes and jewels worn is dazzling to the eyes.'

'But what if we *don't* get noticed?' I asked. 'What if Her Grace passes by and doesn't stop – for she *can't* speak to everyone, can she? What if she's feeling unwell that day, or is of unreasonable temper . . .'

Isabelle put up her hand to stop me. 'Then, if you believe in the worth of the message you bring, you'll have to step forward and seize your chance with her.'

I looked at her in dismay. 'I could never do such a thing!'

'You may have to,' she said, 'or have poor Alice in your head for evermore.'

* * *

We'd hoped to travel to the palace in style, but none of the horses that Isabelle's brother exercised were available on the Sunday, so we had to walk. It was not raining, however (such an occurrence would have been disastrous for our outfits), so Isabelle stepped out early, around seven o'clock, and came along the river path to call for me.

On opening our kitchen door, I stared at her, amazed. 'You look like a real lady!' I said, for though she was only wearing my green gown, she'd borrowed a hat from a neighbour and trimmed it herself with flowers and greenery picked from the hedgerows, and was also wearing a pretty lace shawl, the border of which she'd trimmed with silk ribbons.

'And *you* look very fine, too,' she said, and we gave a low, formal curtsey to each other and burst into giggles.

I was wearing the brown linen bodice and skirt which had been passed to me by Mistress Dee, but Mistress Midge, being something of a seamstress, had shown me how to slash the full sleeves of the bodice and display yellow silk beneath, as was the fashion. I didn't have a hat, alas, but had plaited my hair about my head and pinned it up with some fancy hairpins borrowed from that same lady. Dressed, then, in all our finery, we picked up our skirts and set off.

The walk to the palace took an hour or so along the riverside, and was much enlivened by the 'prentice lads, who left off kicking their footballs in the street to shout after us, or banged on windows as we passed. 'Sweeting! Is it your own wedding you go to, or is there a chance for me yet?' one called, and another whistled long and said, 'I swear I'd die for a kiss from such beauties!'

'And I swear I'll always primp myself up from now on,' Isabelle whispered to me, 'for I've never had as much attention in my life.'

Nearing Richmond Palace, we were surprised by the number of people going in our direction. Not many were in carriages, but there were several in horse-drawn wagons or being carried on litters, and many more on horseback or foot. We looked at all these carefully, judging our own outfits against those of the women and assessing the cut of the doublet, the shape of the leg and the elegance of the young men, and thereby finding several to our liking.

'Have you thought about what you will say if – no, *when* Her Majesty notices you?' Isabelle asked me as the golden towers of the palace came into sight.

I shook my head. 'But if what you think is true and the spirit of Alice Vaizey is speaking through me,' I said, 'then I shall leave it to her. She'll know if and when to speak, and what to say.'

She nodded. 'An excellent notion. And either way, you and I shall have a fine day out and 'twill be something to relate to our families ever after.'

Our families, I thought with a pang, and wondered to myself how Ma was faring and how long it would be before I saw her again.

We both fell silent for a moment as we approached the vast gates with perhaps twenty others, wondering if we might be scrutinised and found lacking in something or other, but the guards – smart in red and purple livery, their steel halberds shining like mirrors – seemed genial enough. 'You good folk will have a long wait,' one of them said, 'for Her Majesty doesn't bestir herself too early on a Sunday morning.'

'About what time d'you think we might see her?' I made bold to ask.

The guard, after looking us up and down and giving a wink of approval, said, 'Eleven o'clock is her usual time to appear in the Presence Chamber.'

I looked at Isabelle, excited and afraid. Just about two hours to wait . . .

As we went through the gates, side-stepping the peddlers selling ribbands and gee-gaws, I looked around me, amazed, for the palace was much, much larger than it appeared from the riverside and was surrounded by many other secondary buildings which I hadn't been able to see before. We were not given long to marvel at the size of it or wonder at the loveliness of the gardens, however, before we were ushered up a flight of marble steps, through two sets of doors and into a long corridor which led to a vast chamber, the largest I could ever have imagined – bigger than the interior of any church I'd ever seen and perhaps as large as those churches which are called cathedrals. Some of the windows were of coloured glass and some plain, but there were a great many of them and the whole place, hung with bright silk flags, looked as you might imagine the interior of a faery castle.

I looked up, and up, for the ceiling was far and away above our heads – and wonder of wonders, it was painted sapphire blue and strewn all over with glittering gold suns, stars and moons.

'Oh – oh!' Isabelle clutched me, awestruck too, and we both stood and stared above us for a while, turning on the spot until, almost dizzy, we were told to move along to make room for all the other petitioners coming into the chamber.

It was all very fine. Great arrangements of flowers and leaves stood high in the window alcoves, and there was a section roped off in the centre of the room with red carpet laid down, while the rest of the floor was strewn with herbs and rushes. More and more people arrived and grouped and regrouped themselves, settling on the floor, adjusting their outfits, re-pinning bodices or smoothing their hair. Some had rolls of parchment, which I supposed were their petitions, while others carried small boxes, and Isabelle and I spent some time speculating on what treasures these might contain, for we'd heard it said that Her Grace was immensely fond of receiving presents of jewellery, so much so that people sometimes ruined themselves in order to buy a fine diamond pin or gem-studded novelty to win her favour.

We settled ourselves as near as we could to the ropes

in order to get the best possible view, and looked around us. The whole effect, as Isabelle had predicted, was astounding, for although there were a few poorer folk in their plain Sunday best, and even one or two Puritans in severe black and white, the women's gowns were mostly vast cartwheels of fine and costly materials: crushed velvet, fine wool, muslin, sarcenet, satin and lace, and in every colour imaginable: magenta, tangerine, scarlet, violet and ochre. Their necks were hung about with necklaces of every type, and most had great ruffs of fine lace which reached past their ears at the back and dipped low in the front, in one case exposing almost the whole of the woman's bosom.

The men were hardly dressed any less flamboyantly, wearing velvet doublets in bright colours – blue or green or scarlet – closed at the front with elaborate frog-fastenings and embroidered all over with flowers. From beneath these jackets silk hose emerged, disappearing in turn into soft leather boots dyed all colours of the rainbow.

Isabelle and I stared about us, almost speechless. So *this* was what the inside of a real palace was like and *this* how the queen's wealthiest subjects displayed themselves. Those huge farthingale skirts worn by the women were the latest styles from Paris.

'Your first time to the palace?' There was a youngish man at my elbow wearing a striking red hat which bore more feathers than a chicken.

'It is,' I said, nodding. 'And yours?'

'Good heavens, no,' he said. 'I am here most Sundays in the hopes that heaven and Her Grace will smile upon me.'

'And has she ever?' Isabelle asked.

'Not yet,' he said. He rolled his eyes and pretended to fan himself. 'But every Sunday I live in hope.'

'And what would happen then?'

'If Her Grace condescends to notice me and I can be droll or witty in my response to her, or sing her a fine song, then she may offer me a position.'

'A place at Court?' I asked. 'But what as?'

'Oh – as anything!' he said airily. 'A lute player, card player, minstrel or poet, or just someone who can turn a fine leg when dancing or impress with his Italian manners. I can do all those things, but have no patron to speak for me, so have to rely on my own cunning.' He patted his velvet doublet, which was in the Tudor colours of red and green, then took off his feathered hat and tucked it underneath his arm. 'I spend my days rehearsing my compliments to the queen, for I mean, come what may, to win her favour.'

'We wish you luck, then,' I said.

He fanned himself again. 'I shall get to Court or die in the attempt!' he declared, and we hardly knew what to reply to this.

The time we spent waiting in that chamber passed in an instant, and indeed I felt that I could have stayed there a whole month and not tired of marvelling at all the fops and fine ladies, and – almost better – those who thought that they were looking magnificent and put on airs and graces, only to draw mocking glances from those around them. Eventually, though, we heard the distant sound of trumpets, and excited whispers passed through the chamber to say that Her Grace was on her way.

Isabelle and I were standing about halfway down the vast chamber and could see along the passageway where we'd come in, which was now also lined with people three or four deep. Those who'd been sitting down to wait now stood up, and then almost immediately began kneeling or bowing their heads in order to receive the queen's blessing as she passed.

The trumpets sounded again. 'I see her!' I said to Isabelle excitedly, straining to see over a hundred heads. 'She's wearing silver and white.'

'A most wonderful dress of silver tissue,' gasped Isabelle, her head bobbing this way and that.

'Her favourite shades,' the young gentleman with the feathered hat said. 'White to symbolise her virginity and silver to emphasise her status.'

'And there are lots of maids of honour!' I said. 'They are two by two following my lady.'

'One of *those* bold misses has recently run off to marry a fortune-hunter,' murmured the young man, who then began pushing his way to the very front, right by the rope, the better to gain the queen's attention.

I didn't take my eyes off Her Grace and saw her

pause several times to speak to different people, and noticed that some of these – a very few – were invited by her to take their places in the train of maids and courtiers that followed behind.

The trumpeters at last sounded a fanfare in the main chamber and I clutched Isabelle's hand, hardly able to draw breath for excitement. As the queen, her farthingale swaying, glided in like a ship in full sail, there was an immediate cry of 'God save Your Majesty!' And the gracious reply came, 'I thank you, my good and loyal citizens.'

There was then a moment's rapt silence before those standing nearest to her began calling out, 'May Your Majesty grant me a position at Court to serve you!' 'Your Grace, please to hear my petition!' 'My good queen! I've worked all my life and am now destitute!' 'Your Majesty, my child will perish without your aid!'

Oh, such things they shouted as would melt the heart of the hardest man! But Her Grace had probably heard them all before and passed most by, nodding courteously, occasionally taking a rolled parchment or accepting one of the gifts, smiling at everyone and saying, 'Bless you, my good people!' as she waved her hand over us in benediction. A few more lucky ones were chosen by her and came from behind the ropes, bursting with pride, to join the little group in her wake.

The queen came closer and I still didn't have a clue in my mind about what I might say, for the intense excitement of being in her presence seemed to have taken everything out of my head. Slowly she moved to stand in front of where we knelt and I began to take in every detail of her appearance. Her ruff flew out each side of her head like the eaves of a house and topped a gown of white and silver tissue, as I'd already observed. Almost every part of the fabric of this gown was covered, *encrusted*, in either embroidery or jewels or both: great pear-shaped pearls, coloured gems, gold chains and precious, glittering diamonds and emeralds. Around her waist she wore a belt of silver and turquoise from which hung a variety of small and exquisite objects: a pomander, silver scissors, some keys, a miniature looking glass and a round object, which I knew to be a pocket watch. The very sight of her was both spectacular and astonishing, and to know that in front of us stood England's queen was the most aston-ishing thing of all.

The befeathered youth, who had moved so far forward that he was standing on the red carpet, called, 'Your Grace! I have composed a song to your beauty!'

The queen stopped and smiled at him, her hair very red in contrast with the icy paleness of her face. 'Then you must certainly come and sing it to us!' she said, her voice clear and light.

'Oh!' Isabelle breathed in my ear. '*Now*, Lucy. Speak while she's near us!'

I opened my mouth, but it was dry with fright and the very notion of speaking to the Queen of England was so daunting that I could not, for the very life of me, utter a single word. I had, perhaps, two seconds in which to act, but this passed in a heartbeat and then Her Grace had gone past us.

'Oh!' I breathed, terribly dismayed. My one chance to be of service to the queen and I hadn't taken it.

Isabelle, seeing my distress, squeezed my hand in sympathy. 'Never mind.'

'I dared not . . .' I began, and then, suddenly, there was a burst of laughter from the passageway and a jester – a flash of yellow silk – came into the Presence Chamber, tumbling over and over in perfect somersaults. The crowd roared and applauded; even the queen turned and smiled at her fool.

He stopped close to where Isabelle and I were standing. He wore a belled cap and a spangled mask across his upper face, but I could still see his eyes, which were a pure and silvery grey.

'Tom-fool!' I breathed.

The jester gave no indication that he'd heard me, but turned away, extending his arm towards Her Majesty. 'How now, Mistress Queen,' he said. 'You have missed two very pretty maids here!'

And Queen Elizabeth turned to look back at her petitioners, saw me and Isabelle and smilingly beckoned to us to join the train behind her . . .

Chapter Seventeen

My legs were shaking as, holding tightly to each other's hands, Isabelle and I joined in the wake of the queen's train as it moved forwards a short way, then stopped so that she could address someone. People in the crowd stared at us with envy and curiosity, no doubt wondering why we were there, and I began to try and work out the answer to this question myself, ready for when I was spoken to by Her Grace.

Isabelle looked at me in wonder. 'Why ever did the jester pick us out?' she asked in a low voice.

'That jester is Tom-fool!' I replied.

'But that's the name of the children's monkey.'

'It is. And the monkey was named after the real fellow, the queen's fool, whose name is actually Tomas. And it was he – remember my tale? – who discovered me in the fireplace at Dr Dee's house.'

'Yes!' Isabelle smiled at me, delighted.

The queen and her train moved on a few steps and then stopped again. 'What shall I say to Her Grace?' I whispered to Isabelle. 'How can I begin to explain? I don't want anyone to think that I have the Sight and condemn me for a wi—'

'Don't say that word here!' Isabelle said swiftly. She thought for a moment. 'You must inform Her Grace that you've dreamed that she's in danger.'

'And not say anything about the occurrence in the churchyard?'

Isabelle shook her head. 'No. I think not.'

I began to rehearse the words in my mind. *Your Grace, I've been having certain dreams . . .* It sounded so insignificant! How could I convey how important I believed my message was?

When Her Grace and her queue of followers had reached the very top of the Presence Chamber, a pair of doors were opened by two guards and we all proceeded into another room. This was smaller than the first, with many portraits and several windowed alcoves, each having a semicircle of cushioned seats. At the back of this room an ornate gilt chair was raised up on a dais, and a little to the right of this was an open door, with two guards in ornate red livery holding their halberds diagonally across the opening. Through this I could see a third chamber, seemingly smaller and more intimate than the one we now stood in.

Without any prompting, people began forming

themselves into little groups. Some of the queen's ladies sat down on cushions and began embroidering, playing games or singing a roundel. There was a harp standing in one of the alcoves, which a lady (named for us as Kat Ashley, Her Grace's most trusted and intimate maid of honour) began playing very sweet and low. Isabelle and I were standing beside an old couple who seemed quite as overawed to be there as we were, and I believe he was petitioning for something, because he had a parchment in his hands and was nervously rolling and unrolling it.

Her Grace moved about the room, listening to what people had to say or introducing them to one or other of the ministers who surrounded her. I looked at these men, wondering if one of them was Robert Dudley, whom everyone spoke of as being remarkably handsome, but although each gentleman was magnificently dressed, I was not sure that one was a deal more comely than the others, for to me they all seemed quite old and venerable. A clerk brought Her Grace a pen and ink and she smilingly signed one or two documents, but other papers she shook her head at, leaving the petitioners to go away, despondent.

I looked anxiously around the room for Tomas and, seeing him juggling a trio of coloured balls at the far end of the room, hoped very much that he would come over; that he hadn't picked me out just to ignore me.

Some moments went by and Her Grace left the side of two petitioners and lifted her hand for the harpist to be silent. She then approached the man in the feathered hat, who stooped so low in his formal bow to her that his nose practically swept the floor. 'You may sing for us,' she said when he straightened up, and he began immediately without any musical accompaniment, kneeling in front of the queen and singing to her with many flourishes and grand gestures. So out of tune was he, though, and so hackneyed the sentiments he conveyed, that it was all everyone could do not to laugh.

Her Grace heard him out and allowed him to kiss her hand, however, then bent and whispered something in his ear which made him blush and smile. He went out backwards, bowing at each step, and I thought how kind a woman she must be to send him on his way with something approaching hope.

It was fully ten minutes more before the queen approached us and as I saw her turn in our direction I froze, terrified that my tongue would cleave to the roof of my mouth again and I'd be unable to speak a word of sense. But it was then that that strange warmth, that odd state of consciousness, came over me, just as it had done in the churchyard, and looking towards the queen as she approached I saw her not as Gloriana, an almost-holy figure, but as a real woman, loved and revered. It was then, also, that I realised that Isabelle was not beside me, and found after that Tomas had led her off to wait in one of the window alcoves.

Her Grace, Queen Elizabeth, moved to stand before me and I sank into a very deep curtsey. She held out a beringed hand to lift me up and, as I raised my eyes, I took in every exacting detail of her appearance. I saw a woman beyond middle age, with age lines at the eyes and mouth, wearing white ceruse on her face which very nearly hid all traces of smallpox scars. Her lips were rouged red, her hairline was high at the front to show a noble forehead, and this was hung with gold chains and a single, blazing ruby. Her hair was piled high, abundant and glossy auburn with not a trace of grey, and plaited all over with pearls.

Tomas appeared, still wearing his eye-mask covered with spangles and with his jester's cap pulled well down and partially covering his face, so I couldn't discern his true appearance (and was still unable to answer for myself the question I'd asked of the girls concerning his looks).

'My right royal lady queen,' he addressed Her Grace, bowing to her from the waist and making the bell on his hat jingle.

The queen turned to regard him. 'Ah, 'tis our fool,' she said, smiling at him fondly.

Tomas dipped his head in acknowledgement. 'By my troth, it's certain that I'm wise enough to play the fool.'

'You wished that we should meet this little maidy,' said the queen.

Tomas turned to look at me. 'Aye,' he said, 'for I knew that if ever she came to Court she'd have something in particular to say, for it's certain she has Your

Grace's well-being at heart.'

I nodded fervently. 'That's true, Your Grace.'

'Then speak, child.'

I took a breath. 'I'm a maid in your magician's house . . .'

'You work for Dr Dee?'

I nodded. 'I look after his children.'

'Good Dr Dee!' She smiled. 'We are persuaded already that you speak for our benefit, for we trust no man as well as he.'

I hesitated. 'I may be speaking of a thing of very little consequence, Your Grace, but feel you should know of a dream which has troubled me of late.'

But the queen seemed preoccupied and certainly didn't seem to take stock of what I was saying. 'As you are of the household of Dr Dee, you must know that he has today sent us a certain elixir,' she said with some gaiety in her voice.

'Today?' I asked, startled. 'He sent something to you *today*?'

She nodded and the three of us began to walk towards the door of what I'd rightly perceived to be part of her privy apartments, the guards raising their halberds and bowing their heads as we went through. This room was much smaller, warm and cosy, with a fire burning in the grate and russet-coloured tapestries on the walls.

The queen went towards a carved oak box on a table. Dr Dee has one of these containing his most valuable books, but when Her Grace lifted the lid of this I saw that it held just one thing: a flask studded all over with precious blue stones: turquoise, sapphire and pale aquamarine. It was a wondrous object, but when I saw it I shivered in my very heart, because it was the flask I'd seen in the show-stone: the one I'd dreamed about.

She lifted it up. 'You will have seen this object before?'

I nodded, spellbound.

She spoke in a low and confidential voice. 'It contains something Dr Dee has long been working on, which we are impatient to take.' She lifted the flask in the air so that the tiny quantity of liquid in the bottom could be seen. 'Such a small amount, but so precious . . .'

My mouth went dry. '*Save my lady!*' I heard Alice Vaizey whisper in my ear.

'Your Grace,' I said, my voice shaking, 'before you drink, surely your taster will try it?'

The queen's eyes clouded over. 'We have no elect taster now, child,' she said, 'since our own dear girl – sweet Alice – died.'

'Alice Vaizey was your taster?' I asked, stunned.

'And now dead,' Tomas said sadly. 'Ah, 'twas never a merry world.'

'Besides,' the queen went on, ''tis such a tiny amount the good doctor has given, that if 'twas tasted there would be none left!' She gave me a tiny smile and I dipped my head. How could I contradict her?

'Fool!' came a sudden cry from outside. 'Come and tumble for us!'

Tomas looked at the queen enquiringly.

'Yes, go to and amuse their Lordships,' she said, waving him off, and Tomas walked backwards out of the room, bowing all the way and turning a somersault at the door.

I knew I must try again. 'You say you received the flask today, Your Grace?'

She looked at me, and nodded.

'For I must tell you that Dr Dee went upriver to Greenwich yesterday and stayed the night. He was not at Mortlake this morning to send you anything.'

But Her Grace had already taken the cork from the jewelled bottle. 'Fie!' she said gaily. 'Perhaps he sent it before he went.'

'But they left straight after breakfast yesterday. There was no time!'

She raised the bottle into the air, turning it and admiring the stones as each caught the light, sparkling and flashing in turn. I don't believe she'd registered what I'd said about Dr Dee's absence, so rapt was she with the bottle, so anxious to drink its contents. 'A costly trinket, this flask,' she said. 'And full worth the value of the liquid which it contains.'

As she spoke I stood transfixed before her, waiting for the inevitable, counting the seconds until she drank that which I believed to be poisoned. She raised the flask to her lips. I watched the royal mouth open, saw the bottle tilt and the stones shimmer, and in my head heard Alice Vaizey scream, '*Save my lady!*'

The words pierced my heart. So insistent was the cry, so anguished, that I could not help but leap forwards and snatch the flask away. 'No!' I screamed. 'Your Grace! It was this flask that I dreamed about!'

There was a shout from one of the guards at the door and a blur of red and gold as they rushed across the room. 'Treason!' one shouted, and the other pushed me so violently from behind that I crashed to the floor, knocking all the air from my body and falling on to my knees so heavily and painfully that I wondered at first if I'd shattered my knee-bones. The flask was snatched from me and I was immediately pulled to my feet again, one guard to each side.

Terrified, I became aware that those in the outer room had gathered to stare at me in horror and – much worse – the queen herself, that beloved monarch I would have died for, was wearing the same disgusted and shocked expression. She stepped back from me, back again, and sunk on to a cushion as if her legs could no longer support her. 'Away,' I heard her say shakily. 'Take her away . . .'

The guards hauled me out one at each arm, dragging me behind them like a market coster dragging a sack of potatoes, and I just had time to see Tomas's face registering incredulity, and that of Isabelle, her mouth open in a wide 'O' of shock. Distressed, weeping, I was bumped down two flights of stairs, hauled across a cellar and pulled in and out of dark spaces, then flung into a wet and cold room, where the door was slammed behind me. I say room, but it had none of the usual comforts of such a place: no furniture, nor window to let in the light, only a small, barred opening too high to see out of. It was, in fact, a dungeon.

I wept for long minutes, frightened beyond words about what might happen to me. I well knew the penalty for touching the person of the queen, and though I'd committed this offence for a true and honest reason, had heard tales of citizens taken to the Tower and tortured into making confessions that weren't true, just to have that torture cease. Moreover, I was sorely worried that Her Grace might drink some of that elixir.

I forced myself to stop weeping and dried my face on my gown, then roused myself sufficiently to hobble to the door (for my knees were paining me) and began banging on it. 'Let me out!' I shouted, 'Let me out!' over and over again, until my knuckles felt raw and my voice changed to sobs again.

I slumped on to the floor, momentarily defeated, then heard the skitter of a rat and got up to begin banging again. 'There are rats!' I screamed, but heard no reply, just my voice echoing through empty spaces. I began to pace up and down as well as I could, partly to keep myself warm, partly to try and scare off vermin by my continual movements. As I walked, I shouted, so didn't hear the approach of anyone until a grille in the door was slid across and the red nose and grizzled grey beard of one of the palace guards appeared.

'What is it? You'll be fed when they thinks of it,' a gruff voice said.

'I don't want food!' I cried, for that was the last thing on my mind. 'I must speak to someone. I must speak to the queen's fool!'

'Ho!' the voice jeered. 'Must you now?'

I heard the grille scrape as he began to close it, and spoke up again quickly. 'Please! I've something to give you!'

'What's that, then?' he asked, sudden interest in his voice.

I felt under my bodice, for I'd hidden my groat on entering the palace, knowing how such a thing would look amid all the real gold and silver that we'd see. 'It's this,' I said, lifting off my keepsake. 'Please take it to the queen's fool – to Tomas, if you know him – to remind him that I am Her Grace's most faithful and loving servant and will be for evermore.' I pushed the groat through the grille as I spoke and saw him look at it with some scorn. 'I know 'tis only a humble thing, but it stands for much. And would you please also tell Tomas this: that he must have the elixir tested by an apothecary before the queen takes it. He must!'

'Eh?' said the guard, and I wondered how much of what I'd said he had understood.

'Please!' I implored him. 'Tomas will see that you're rewarded!'

This he did seem to understand, and he took the groat and closed the window without saying any more. 'He must have the elixir tried!' I called after, praying that he'd somehow sense the urgency of what I was saying and not just steal the groat for the paltry sum it was worth.

I waited longer then, alternately pacing and weeping as before, and after what seemed an age heard footsteps outside and the bolt being drawn across.

When the door opened it was Tomas who stood there, and so thankful was I to see him that it was all I could do to stop myself flinging my arms about him and hanging on his neck. 'What is it? What's happened?' I asked urgently.

He smiled at me gravely. 'We have discovered that the flask contained hemlock.'

I gasped.

'Hemlock,' he repeated, 'with its pretty flowers of white lace and its power to stop the heart.'

'But the queen did not . . . ?'

'She did not.'

My eyes filled with tears and my relief was so great that I sagged against the wall.

'She was still thinking on it, but I was against it. And when I received your token I persuaded Her Grace to try the elixir first on someone who was rather more expendable than the Queen of England.'

'And was there such a person?' I asked, rather shocked.

'Not a person, but a yellow canary owned by one of the ladies-in-waiting.'

'It died?'

'It did. One sip and it fell down with its claws in the air.'

'I knew it,' I said, my voice shaking.

'But how did you know?'

I looked at him, suddenly embarrassed. 'I dreamed it.'

'Ah,' he nodded.

'And what did Her Grace do then – when it became clear that the flask did contain poison?'

'She went exceeding pale and had to be revived from a faint.'

I gasped again.

'But – thanks be – she has the stamina and heart of a lion and recovered quickly, thanks to the ministrations of her ladies and a little oil of lavender applied to her temples.' He smiled. 'And thanks be to you, of course.' He delved in a pocket, then held out my groat to me, looking at it with some amusement. 'And here is your precious coin back again.'

He held it up ready to tie about my neck, and as his fingers touched my skin, I shivered.

'Are my hands cold?' he asked.

I was about to say no, but then in case he realised I was shivering for quite another reason, mumbled, 'A little,' and felt myself blush. To cover my confusion, I asked if they'd discovered where the elixir had really come from.

He nodded. 'It was delivered to Her Grace by a girl named Cicily, a new lady-in-waiting, who announced that it had been handed to her by a trusted servant of Dr Dee.'

I could not but smile. 'Our household *has* no servants!'

'But when we looked for her, little Cicily couldn't be found sewing or dancing or playing games . . .'

'She'd gone?'

Tomas clapped his hands in the manner of a magician completing a trick. 'She had disappeared. And when Kat Ashley was sent to Cicily's bedchamber she discovered that her gowns had also vanished and her room was bare. But not completely bare: she'd left behind her a tract putting forward the supposedly superior claim to the throne of the queen's cousin, the Queen of Scotland.'

'Then it was this Cecily who . . .'

Tomas nodded. 'She was acting in the pay of someone else, of course: someone far more important and powerful. We may or may not find out who that someone was.'

I'd composed myself by then, dried my eyes on my kerchief, smoothed my hair and straightened my skirts, so was ready when Tomas offered his arm to walk back through the cellars which I'd been dragged across some time before. 'So you are quite convinced that Her Grace knows of my complete innocence?'

Tomas nodded. 'She does. And she's very grateful

for your prompt action. So much so, that I think you may hear word from her soon.'

I blushed. 'My only wish would be to serve her faithfully.'

'I know that,' said Tomas, 'and there may well be a means whereby you can do this to greater effect.'

My heart started beating very fast, for of course this could only mean that she was going to take me into her service. 'Truly?'

'Truly,' Tomas said. 'Her Grace has a foreign ambassador with her now, but you'll hear from her soon. And in the meantime I'm to escort you to the outer chamber, where your friend Isabelle is waiting for you – and has, I believe, already made the acquaintance of a fine young footman. You can walk home, and each tell the other of your day's adventures . . .'

I smiled at him, barely taking notice of his words. To enter the queen's service, to become one of her ladies-in-waiting. It was all I'd ever dreamed of . . .

Chapter Eighteen

I was sent out to market early the next morning, for Mistress Midge had a mind to prepare a feast to welcome back the master and mistress from Greenwich and was even contemplating opening up the dining room. It hadn't been hard to keep what had happened a secret from her, for when I'd arrived home late the previous afternoon I'd found her sprawled at the kitchen table, drunk, her face flat down in a porringer, and that morning she hadn't even seemed to recall that I'd gone to the palace at all.

I yawned as I walked along, for, overexcited, I'd spent most of the night wide awake and reliving every moment of the day that had passed, scarce able to believe what had happened: at the way we'd been chosen out of the glittering crowd; at the audacious manner I'd leaped at the queen to take the flask from her hands; at how I'd been thrown into the dungeon;

and – finally and most magnificently – how Tomas had thanked me on behalf of the queen and told me that Her Grace would send word to me. How soon could I begin working for her? I wondered. What tasks might I be called upon to perform? I was a little worried by the fact that I had few accomplishments – although I could read fairly well now – but believed I might be taught about music, dancing, singing and the like.

At the market, Isabelle was selling fresh garlic and had a goodly crop of plump and juicy bulbs in her wooden trug. She was yawning, too, though, and hardly bothering to cry up her produce, so that the housewife next to her, also selling garlic, was getting all the business.

She perked up as I sat down beside her. 'You've come at last!'

''Tis not late.'

''Tis when you've spent a sleepless night.'

'Thinking of your footman?' I teased her.

'Thinking that I might have had to rescue you from the Tower!' she retorted, and we smiled at each other and clasped hands.

'Everything went through my head over and over . . .'

'But did you have the dream again? The one with Mistress Vaizey?'

'I hardly slept enough to dream.' I thought about it for a moment and then realised. 'But no, I didn't have *that* dream, the one where the queen was dead.'

She shushed me and I clapped my hand to my mouth, for, of course, to discuss such matters as the death of the queen was treason.

A group of housewives passed us. 'Fresh garlic!' Isabelle cried, making some effort. 'New young garlic!' No one paid any attention to her, however, so she turned back to me. 'What will happen now, do you think? How long will it be before you're called to the palace?'

'I hope not too long,' I said with some excitement.

'And you do think that you'll have to live there . . .'

I nodded assuredly, for we'd discussed this on the way home the previous afternoon and I'd come to the conclusion that all the queen's ladies-in-waiting would have to live wherever she was, ready to attend upon her at all times. 'I will surely have to be where the Court is, ready to be with the queen on her progresses through the country.'

Isabelle looked at me wistfully. 'Then I'll miss you very much.'

'Perhaps you can visit me,' I said with some uncertainty, for I wasn't at all sure of the etiquette for such an event.

'Will you have your own room, do you think?'

'Surely! And a generous dress allowance, for the queen's ladies can't be seen to be less than fashionable. I've heard – for a great lady in Hazelgrove used to be at Whitehall Palace – that a woman is employed just to do their hair, and that if you're a maid of honour, which is the best sort of lady-in-waiting, then you have your own maid!'

'Oh,' said Isabelle, rather despondently. 'But won't you be sad to leave Beth and Merryl?'

'I will, but I'll come back and see them,' I said. 'And I'll come back and see you, too.'

But this didn't seem to raise her spirits. 'You'll forget about me,' she said sadly. 'You'll make fine new friends, *ladies*, and forget all about me.'

'Of course I won't,' I said, but to be truthful, I'd been wondering that myself. I'd miss Isabelle, of course, and the two little girls and even Mistress Midge, but the excitement of Court life would more than make up for that.

At market I obtained all the foodstuffs that Mistress Midge had requested, including a fine, plump goose, which I swung over my shoulder, and was humming for sheer joy as I stepped out for home. As I crossed the lane and passed the porch of St Mary's, however, a dark-hooded figure stepped out of the shadows. Grasping my arm, he pulled me into the porch.

'Alms, Madam!' he croaked. 'Aid a poor beggar who has only recently survived a horrid and contagious disease . . .'

Giving a little scream of fright, I tried to brush off the hand that held me, but the beggar's grip was surprisingly strong. 'Let me go!' I cried out. 'I carry no money!'

'Then give me that fine goose you're carrying, I pray you,' came the cracked reply, 'for in the pest house they feed you such amounts as 'twould hardly keep a dormouse alive.'

'These aren't my provisions,' I said. 'They belong to my master and mistress and they'll beat me if I come home without them.'

The grip tightened somewhat. 'Then you must tell them you were waylaid by a disease-ridden old beggar who threatened to harm you unless you gave him your fine goose – and a kiss.'

'A kiss!' I cried, horrified, thinking that I'd have given him my whole basket of goods and taken the consequences rather than kiss whatever plague-ravaged face lay beneath the filthy cowl.

'Is't so repugnant, Mistress?' He stood, bent of back, his head on one side and looked up at me, but I could see very little of his features, for the porch was dark and overhung by a vast yew tree.

I strained my eyes to see what I didn't want to see. Was that a plague sore on his cheek? Trembling, I tried to temper my reaction, for I didn't wish to provoke him. I even tried to smile, but made little success of it.

He drew me closer to him. 'Would you deny a kiss to a poor old man who's near death?'

'I . . . I . . .'

'Or would you, mayhap, prefer to kiss the queen's fool?'

I gasped. 'What do you mean?'

There was sudden laughter in his voice. ''Tis I, Tomas,' he said. He straightened up and his hold on my wrist became looser; one that caressed rather than gripped. 'Forgive me, Lucy,' he said. 'I came here in disguise and – such is my devotion to my trade – couldn't resist playing a jape.'

I snatched back my hand. ''Twas not a jape!' I said. ''Twas cruel and I was frightened. Besides, 'tis too early in the day for fooling.'

''Tis never too early. Though the hour's but small, my wit is like the marigold and opens with the sun.'

''Tis not at all sunny today,' I said obstinately.

His hand came to rest on my shoulder. 'Lucy, I am sorry. Truly,' he said. 'Being in Court, where all is bluff and artifice, I sometimes forget the ordinary sensibilities.'

I looked up, under his hood, and could see little but his grey eyes shining and his mouth curved in a smile.

'Then . . . then if you are truly sorry, will you take your hood off and let me see you properly?'

'I cannot,' he said, 'for I come in disguise for a reason.'

My heartbeat steadying now, I looked at him with growing interest. It must, surely, be something to do with my elevation to Court. Perhaps he was going to tell me that I must go with him now and begin my new responsibilities.

He glanced about us to see that we were not being observed. 'I talked with Her Grace long into the night,' he said, seeming to confirm my expectations, 'and with Kat Ashley and Sir Thomas Walsingham also.'

'The queen's spymaster?' I asked, puzzled.

'Yes. But the talk went no further than we four, for Her Grace does not wish her loyal subjects to know how close she was to taking poison without knowing it.' His voice dropped as he added, 'Or how close England came to being without a ruler.'

I nodded wordlessly.

'We talked of you and how you should be rewarded.'

I felt myself flush. 'I seek no other reward but to serve Her Grace,' I said again.

'Quite so. And thus the queen has sent me here this morning to make you a proposition.'

'Truly?' Before I could stop myself, I burst out, 'Tell me, then, when am I to become a lady-in-waiting?'

Much to my discomfiture, he began laughing. 'A lady-in-waiting? No, I fear you are not to become one of those.'

'*Not?*' I looked at him in dismay.

'Dear Lucy, you'd be unhappy in such a situation, for the women who surround the queen are of the type who seek preferment at every turn and can kick like a she-ass if they think anyone is usurping their position.'

'Oh,' was all I could say, and it was hard to stop my bottom lip from jutting out childishly.

He put his hand on my arm, 'They are titled girls,' he said gently, 'highly educated and very aware of their place in life. They use the Court as a marriage market, each vying one with another for the best catch.'

'So just because I don't have a title . . .' I began, tears coming into my eyes.

'And thank God you do *not* have a title, for the queen wants you to take on a more exacting role.'

I looked at him as well as I could, for his face was still concealed under his hood. 'And what is that?'

'Her Grace wants you to spy for her.'

'Spy for her?' I repeated disbelievingly.

'To *observe*, shall we say? For that doesn't sound so alarming.' He squeezed my arm. 'She knows that Dr Dee is of loyal heart, but fears that those who surround him may be of lesser mettle. Her Grace wants to know what people are saying about her in the streets and in marketplaces, in church and at hiring fairs and bear-baitings. She wants to know, in short, what is the true opinion of the people. If there is any dissent to her rule she wants to hear of it; if there is sympathy for her cousin Mary and the old religion then she wishes to be privy to that, too.'

'And how would I discover such things?'

'Just by going about your normal business in Dr Dee's household and keeping your eyes and ears open. And, in addition, sometimes I may point you in a certain direction and ask you to give your observations on a particular person.'

'And would Dr Dee know of all this?'

Tomas shook his head. 'He would not. As few

people as possible should know. Her Grace will devise some little assignments which will make it necessary for you to come and go between Mortlake and wherever the Court may be, so that your occasional presence is not remarked upon.'

'So . . . so I won't be the queen's lady-in-waiting?'

'No. You'll remain Dr Dee's servant, a reliable but simple girl going about her duties. No one would suspect such a person and all would speak freely in front of one.'

I sighed. 'But I so longed to be at Court.'

He squeezed my hand. 'The Court is like the stage, Lucy. All are players and all is false. Remember that when you pass through it.'

'But will I be seeing you sometimes?'

'Undoubtedly.' He laughed. 'But whether you will recognise me is another matter.'

He raised my hand to his lips, kissed my palm and folded my fingers over the kiss, one by one. 'Keep this safe until I see you again,' he said. And was gone.

Thoughtfully, I continued my journey back to the magician's house. My life was changing, although not as I'd wished. 'Twould, however, be an interesting change . . .

A Note from the Author on the Cast of Characters

෨෧

I have deliberately not given a firm date for the happenings in this book but it is set sometime during the start of the second half of Elizabeth I's reign, when the queen was in her early forties. At this time her ministers had not given up hope that she might marry and even, perhaps, provide the heir that England so needed. There was much public speculation about who might or might not be one of the queen's lovers. Robert Dudley, Earl of Leicester, was her long-term favourite, but many a young dandy spent a fortune on clothes and fancy accessories in his attempts to be noticed by her. The queen's courtship by the French Duke of Alencon went on for several years and they even exchanged rings, but the fact that she was Protestant and he Catholic (and also a foreigner) eventually went against him.

Many of the other people mentioned in this book were real: Walsingham, Kelly, Robert Dudley – and Dr John Dee, of course. Dee was a brilliant mathematician, map-maker, linguist and scholar – but he also appears to have been very gullible. Kelly, his 'scryer', purported to have had conversations with several spirits who gave information on how to turn metal into gold, but unfortunately, these instructions were in a complicated angelic language and could never be properly deciphered. Every philosopher/scientist of the time was searching for the 'philosopher's stone', which would turn base metals into gold and bring about everlasting life. Certain magical items belonging to Dr Dee are on show in the British Museum, and there is a pen and ink drawing made at the time, which purports to show Dee and Kelly in the churchyard at Mortlake, speaking to a spirit Dee has raised.

People were very superstitious in the sixteenth and seventeenth centuries and astrology was a legitimate science. Those families who could afford it would have had a chart cast at the birth of a child to see what fate had in store. Dr Dee was consulted about the most auspicious coronation date for Queen Elizabeth, and she visited his house in Mortlake several times.

Unfortunately, nothing now remains of Dee's house and library (once said to be the biggest private library in the country), only a wall in the churchyard, which is said to have led into his garden. Little remains, either, of Richmond Palace, except a picturesque archway and some ancient walls.

Lucy is, of course, a fictional character, but Dr Dee and his family would have had servants and it is fascinating to speculate what they might have thought of him and his magical endeavours. Dr Dee lived a long life, had two wives and eight children, but never achieved the great fame and riches he so desired. He died, almost penniless, in 1608 when he was eighty-one.

Queen Elizabeth had several jesters and fools over her lifetime. These lived at court mainly to make her laugh and lighten her duties, although some were *wise* fools who would, in seeming to talk nonsense, actually give good advice. One of her favourite jesters was Thomasina, a female dwarf, who accompanied Elizabeth on her many progresses throughout the country. Then there was Monarcho, an Italian fool, and the Greens: a whole family of jesters. As the queen also had a network of spies working under Sir Francis Walsingham, it doesn't seem to be stretching credulity too far to suggest that Tomas could have been a jester *and* a spy.

There were many attempts on Elizabeth's life and most of these derived from the supporters of the Catholic Mary, Queen of Scots. She had a good claim to the English throne being, like Elizabeth, a granddaughter of Henry VII. In 1585, Anthony Babington's coded correspondence with Mary was deciphered by Sir Francis Walsingham's spy network, revealing a complex plan to unseat Elizabeth and put Mary on the throne of England. These attempts increased, sometimes involving foreign powers, until Elizabeth reluctantly signed Mary's death warrant in 1587.

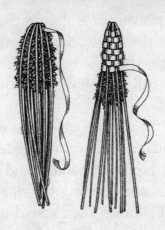

How to Make
Lavender Wands

Use at least thirteen (it should be an odd number) of long stems of fresh lavender, not dried, and two or three metres (the amount will depend on the length of your stalks) of narrow coloured ribbon in whatever colour you choose.

1. Make a bunch of the lavender stems, lining them up at the *base* of the flower heads rather than the tops of the flowers.

2. With the ribbon, carefully tie the stems together just below the heads, leaving one end of ribbon much longer than the other, although the shorter end must still be longer than the length of the flower heads.
3. Gently bend back each stem surrounding the flower heads until they are completely enclosed, as if in a cage, keeping the longer end of the ribbon on the outside, and allowing the shorter end to hang down in the 'cage'. Then spread the stalks so that they are evenly spaced around the flowers.
4. Taking the longer end of the ribbon, weave it under and over each stem in turn, using firm and even movements and pulling the stems fairly tight, until you run out of flowers to cover.
5. Tie a firm knot at the base of the 'cage' with both ends of the ribbon, and finish with a bow.

Hung in your wardrobe, this wand will make your clothes smell sweet and deter moths.

Glossary

bruisewort – a plant supposed to heal bruises, such as ox-eyed daisy or comfrey

caudle – hot spiced wine drink made with gruel, egg yolk, oatmeal, etc. sometimes used a medicine

ceruse – a white lead pigment used as makeup

chafing dish – portable brazier to hold burning coals; dishes of food could be reheated on it

coffer – a box or chest for keeping valuables

coster – someone who sells fruit or vegetables from a barrow or stall

coxcomb – a foppish fellow; a conceited dandy

equerry – an officer in the royal household

ewer – a pitcher with a wide spout and handle for pouring

flummeries – cold puddings, sweet and bland, made with oatmeal or flour

frowsy – unkept; of shabby appearance

gee-gaw – decorative trinket; a bauble

goldcups – old name for buttercup or crowfoot plant

Groat – English silver coin worth four old pence, used from the 14th century to the 17th century

harridan – a woman with a reputation for being a scold or a nag

horn book – Early primer showing alphabet, etc. consisting of a wooden board protected by a thin sheet of cattle horn

jumbales – small flat ring-shaped cakes or cookies

kirtle – the skirt part of a woman's outfit. During this time everything (skirt, bodice, sleeves, ruff) came separately and were pinned together during dressing

litter – a man-powered form of transport, consisting of a chair or couch enclosed by curtains and carried on a frame or poles

lye – a cleansing solution traditionally made from wood ash and 'bedchamber urine'

lying-in – the period just before and after a woman's confinement during childbirth

medlars – fruit of deciduous tree similar to an apple, now little grown

neocromancer – sorcerer, black magician. One who tries to conjure up the dead

pipkin – small metal or earthenware vessel

porringer – a shallow dish or cup, usually with a handle, and used for eating soup, stews or porridge

posset – a drink of hot milk curdled with ale or beer, flavoured with spices; a common recipe for treating colds

pribbling – an insulting term

prinked up – to dress oneself finely; to deck out and preen oneself

puttock – an insulting term

Rhenish – a dry white wine

ribband – a ribbon

samite – a heavy silken fabric, often woven with gold or silver threads

sarcenet – fine soft silk fabric used for clothing and ribbons

scabious – field flower with round heads of pale blue flowers, thought effectual for treating coughs

scry – to see or divine, especially by crystal-gazing

simples – medicines made from herbs

tansy – yellow-flowered plant related to dandelion; used for cleaning the skin of discolouration

tinctures – medicinal extract in a solution of alcohol

trencher – wooden or pewter plate for serving or cutting food

trug – long shallow basket for carrying flowers or fruit

vittles – food; also spelled *victuals*

wool-carder – someone who combs the wool in order to align the fibres before weaving

Bibliography

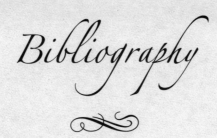

Elizabeth the Queen, Alison Weir
Pimlico, 1999

The Life and Times of Elizabeth, Neville Williams
Book Club Associates, 1972

Elizabeth the Great, Elizabeth Jenkins
Phoenix Press, 1958

John Dee 1527-1608, Charlotte Fell Smith
Constable and Company, 1909

Barnes and Mortlake Past, Maisie Brown
Historical Publications Limited, 1997

The Gentlewoman's Companion, Hannah Woolley (1675)
Prospect Books, 2001

Elizabeth's London, Liza Picard
Phoenix, 2003

Our first glimpse of the frost fair came just as dusk was falling and the air was soft and misty all around. Viewed under these conditions any place can take on a kind of enchantment, but to come around the bend in the river, to hear music playing and see the fair from a distance, lit at each side of the river by huge baskets of burning coals, was truly a glimpse of a kind of faeryland ...

Find out what the future holds for Lucy in the follow-up to
At the House of the Magician ...

BY ROYAL COMMAND

OUT NOW

Turn the page to find out more . . .

BY ROYAL COMMAND

Available Now

**The Queen, the Spy and the Fool
in a Tale of Romance and Royal Conspiracy**

Lucy has been waiting to be given an assignment which
will assist the queen – and she's anxious, too, to see
Tomas again. When she takes Beth and Merryl to the
frost fair on the Thames, she speaks to Tomas and gets
the news she's been waiting for: she has been requested
to go to Court and watch closely one Mistress
Madeleine Pryor, who is suspected of being in league
with Elizabeth's great rival: Mary, Queen of Scots.

This also means, of course, that Lucy must attend
various glittering occasions, mingle with the maids
of honour and, above all, try to keep her real
identity a secret . . .

www.maryhooper.co.uk

Sequel to At The Sign of The Sugared Plum

Petals in the Ashes

MARY HOOPER